James Francis Clarke kept doing things. He kept making Samantha cry, and he kept on kissing her! He just had this strange effect on everything. On her, on Mom, on Grampa, on Vicky ... and especially on bridges!

THE TROUBLE WITH BRIDGES

BY

EMMA GOLDRICK

MILLS & BOON LIMITED
15–16 BROOK'S MEWS
LONDON W1A 1DR

First published in Great Britain 1985
by Mills & Boon Limited

© Emma Goldrick 1985

Australian copyright 1985
Philippine copyright 1985
This edition 1985

ISBN 0 263 75086 8

Set in Monophoto Times 10 on 10 pt.
01-0785 – 61551

Made and printed in Great Britain by
Richard Clay (The Chaucer Press) Ltd,
Bungay, Suffolk

With apologies to
a dear old Bridge.

CHAPTER ONE

SHE was completely out of breath when she ran up the stone stairs leading into the Municipal Building. The corridor was half-full of impatient city employees racing out for lunch, and the lift was not worth waiting for. She ran for the stairs, slipping on the ancient floor. A policeman stood outside the entrance to the Council Chamber, where the press conference was scheduled. He put one long arm across the open doorway and stopped her.

'Too late, kid,' he told her as she tried in vain to duck under his arm. 'Only members of the press.'

'That's me,' she squeaked as she fumbled through her canvas holdall for her press-pass.

'I mean the working press,' he insisted. 'Not you high school kids. Did you cut a class or something?'

'Darn you,' she muttered, fully aware that her five-foot frame, her straw-coloured plaits, and her well-worn denim skirt all added up much too easily to his conclusion. And then her fumbling hand found the plastic card. At the bottom, of course. Underneath Vicky's bronzed baby shoe, the little knit top that she had promised to mend and ten thousand other items, all crucial to her existence—whenever she could find them.

She pulled out the card and triumphantly flashed it in his face. And then, with the briefing at least half-finished, he insisted on reading it! I'll kill him, she told herself!

She could hear the voices from the front of the room, but the words were indecipherable. She bounced up on tiptoes, hoping to get a view of whatever it was that was going on up front, but her luck was still running badly.

'Okay,' the policeman said, sounding as if he regretted having to let her in. 'Although why the Providence *Gazette* would send a kid like you . . .' He scratched the back of his head, peered into the room, and gestured. 'There's a few seats in the back row,' he said, 'but the briefing is almost finished.'

And I hope you catch a terminal case of dandruff, she muttered under her breath as she squeezed by him and into the first aisle seat she could find. She flipped on her tape-recorder, knowing already it was a lost cause without the special long-distance microphone. Which, as usual, she had left lying on her bed in the mad rush to get Vicky up and fed, her mother into her wheelchair and bathed. It's a conspiracy, she told herself. Somebody up there is out to get me!

She leaned as far forward as space would allow, peering around the big man in front of her, using the aisle as a viewing zone. Two men were standing at the front of the room, by a display table. She recognised the older one as John Prichard, the political appointee who headed the State Department of Public Works. He was an old pro, six feet tall, with distinguished white hair, and just the slightest protuberance at the beltline. He was flashing his perfectly capped teeth now at a question she had missed. She took a quick look at the other man. Younger, leaner, just as tall. There was something—an aura—around him. A look of friendly competence. And a lovely smile! As if reading her mind he stepped aside, and nodded his head towards the model on the table-top.

'... and we at the Statehouse,' the politician was saying, 'mean to do everything in our power to get this new bridge built with great speed, and with as little inconvenience as is possible.' There was a scattering of applause from the first row, where the party hacks were seated.

Of course, she reminded herself. It's an election year. Every fourth year, down they come with a new model of a bridge that will solve all our problems. It will wipe out the eighty-year-old swing bridge across the mouth of the Acushnet River, and make the world safe for democracy. Sure it will! Her pencil scratched at her notebook, getting a brief description of the proposed high-rise suspension span being proposed. A picture would have saved the trouble, she knew, but the metropolitan paper for which she worked had no use for pictures from stringers—local part-time reporters who were called in where no regular reporter would ever consider going. And besides, if she worked all night and turned out a thousand-word masterpiece, Rewrite would cut it down to two or three lines at best!

'How soon is that?'

The politician looked at the questioner as if he were deliberately sabotaging the show. 'Well, you know that bridge-building is a very complex affair. Let's say, to be on the safe side—three years?'

'More than likely seven,' the young man at his side interjected. He received a glower for his pains. Mr Prichard continued on. 'You know how engineers tend to be over-cautious. You can count on me. Three years. Are there any more questions?' He had an undertaker's look on his face—the one that indicated he would be *very* surprised if any of his customers talked back!

Samantha waited a suitable time for her elders to get in their questions, but when none eventuated she stood up and waved her hand. Nobody noticed. 'Darn,' she muttered. It was the penalty one pays for being a shortie in a tall world, she knew. With an additional word or two from her grandfather's vocabulary she hitched up her denim wrap-around skirt and climbed up on her folding chair, still waving her hand. At least the young man noticed. He flashed her a broad gleaming smile—and just for a second frozen in time it struck her how nice that smile was. How very nice! He said something in the politician's ear.

'The little girl in the back. You have a question?'

It was all delivered in his *Motherhood*, *God* and *Country* voice. Look at me, it yelled. The busy keeper of the States's treasures, condescending to answer the inane question of some kid-reporter. And the tone, more than the words, set off Samantha Clark's short fuse.

'Tell me,' she almost yelled. 'While the State takes

from three to seven years to build the new bridge, how do we local citizens get back and forth over the river?'

There was a flurry of laughter from the usually cynical press corps. Mr Prichard turned slightly red, then regained his aplomb. 'That's a silly question,' he pontificated. 'Which newspaper do you represent?' From her wobbly perch Samantha could read very clearly the message his body was sending. *I don't have to make a statement to some kid from the East Freetown Ledger!* But when she gave him the prestigious name of her paper, his whole attitude changed.

'Oh, the *Gazette*.' He cleared his throat grumpily. 'At the beginning of our press conference we talked about that. There is nothing essentially wrong with the present bridge. After all, it's only eighty years-old. It's a good, dependable old lady. Of course we'll spend a little money repairing it. It does need some minor up-dating. But yes, we'll keep the old bridge in service, young lady. And if you had come on time you would have heard the details.'

'Yes, well——' For some reason Samantha's chair seemed to be jiggling more than one would expect. It distracted her attention completely. The young man up front was hurrying up the aisle, and her chair was rocking, teetering on the edge. 'I—help!' Her scream misfired, and came out as a squeak, the appeal hardly noticed even in the row of men directly in front of her. The chair rocked from side to side twice. She could see catastrophy staring her in the face, and was unable to do anything about it. A newspaper headline flashed across her mind: 'Impertinent *Gazette* Reporter Killed in Chair Crash.' And then another thought. This afternoon is Vicky's birthday, and if I miss the party she'll kill me!

By this time the chair was oscillating from side to side in wild abandon, and, unable to sustain herself, Samantha gave up and jumped, just as the chair swerved towards the aisle.

Expectations are often wildly incorrect. Samantha closed her eyes, trusting to providence that her landing would do little more than bruise her pert posterior. Instead, she failed to land at all. That is to say, her downward plunge was deftly terminated in a pair of masculine arms, which then proceeded to squeeze her gently, and hug her closely. Cautiously she opened one eye.

Right in front of her was the bronzed face of the young man who had taken part in the briefing. So close as to be almost out of focus to a girl who was long-sighted, and required reading glasses. Interesting! She managed to pry the other eye open. That big smile flashed across his face. Look at that, Sam thought disgustedly. Blond curly hair. And I spend two nights a week trying to get my hair to curl! Damn man! Blue eyes, too. The kind you could drown in. Heavy eyebrows, that cast shadows. He needs a shave, no less, but smell the—the niceness of him, will you! This is altogether too much!

'You could put me down now,' she suggested defensively. 'Unless the laws of gravity have been amended, I'm finished falling.'

'Oh—well . . .' There was an upturned corner to his mouth, a sort of suppressed laugh. 'I would if I could. But the cause of your accident is still there. And it's all my fault, of course.'

'Of course,' she muttered angrily. Of course it's your fault. Whose else? What in the world is he talking about? There was a change in the noise level of the room. Reporters, most bored to tears, were struggling to get out the narrow doors of the conference room.

He stepped carefully out of the aisle to avoid the rush, still holding her gently in his arms, as if her 105 pounds meant nothing at all. She found it hard not to stare. He was so—close. So damnable masculine. Not quite as tall as she had thought, perhaps. *Tall enough for me*, her scandalous subconscience interjected. But Lord, feel those muscles. And a dimple. Can you imagine that? Blue eyes, curly blond hair, and a dimple. God was trying to mock the whole race of women when SHE designed this one!

'I think you can safely put me down now,' she

suggested. Before I'm overwhelmed by the whole affair and bite you—or something! He looks like a pirate. A blond pirate. Do they still abduct their women, and carry them screaming into the ships? I'd better practise my screaming, just in case! 'You could put me down?'

'Oh—down! Yes, yes of course. I'd forgotten!'

'You'd forgotten?'

'I—a figure of speech. You make a nice armful of woman. I thought—well, the crowd has gone, and if we can get her to move——' He bent over slightly searching the floor at their feet.

'Her?'

'My dog.'

'That's a dog?' A great white hairy mass of animal was squirming out from under the area where her chair had collapsed. There seemed to be neither head nor tail, just a tremendous mass of white squirming hair. One end wiggled.

'Yes. My dog.' He was very solemn about the affair. So much so that Samantha repressed her giggles. 'My prize English Sheep Dog. She has a problem. Runaway genes, or something like that. She never seems to stop growing. And at a hundred pounds a stupid sheep dog is hard to handle. She was hiding under your chair. Large crowds frighten her.'

'Jim! Jim!' Still clinging, Sam looked over his shoulder. Prichard, the politician, was standing impatiently in the aisle. 'Can you stay here and see what you can do? I have to get back to the Statehouse for a conference with the governor. Is that your damn dog in trouble again?'

'Yes, Mr Prichard, that's my damn dog. My landlady won't let me leave him alone in my apartment.'

'You'll play the devil trying to find a hotel down here that will let you keep her, either.' Mr Prichard seemed to savour the problem his assistant would have. He licked at his lips, then inspected Samantha. 'Nice,' he added. 'Something local you picked up?'

'Fell right into my arms,' the younger man responded. In just a minute, Samantha thought, in just a little minute, I'm going to pound them both in the mouth. What do they think I am? Something delivered in the mail? Male chauvinists, both of them. 'Put me down,' she hissed.

'Down? Yes, of course. Move over, dog.' His foot gently nudged the animal aside, and he set Samantha down on her feet.

'Well . . .' she spluttered, unable for the moment to think of an appropriate statement. And for the first time in her life, for want of the proper word, she said nothing. He had set her down directly in front of him, then stepped back half a pace, with a hand on each of her shoulders. She was frantically trying to re-arrange her wrap-around skirt, which had been twisted all out of position by the accident. And then she realised just what he was doing. With a great deal of care and attention he was slowly scanning her, like a radar set, from head to toe. Across her straw-coloured plaits, the heart-shaped Irish face, the grey-green eyes, the stubborn chin. And then down her tiny frame, hovering hungrily at the pert swell of her breasts, the tiny waist, the burgeoning hips.

'Well?' she snapped at him furiously.

'Very well indeed,' he returned placidly. 'Nice.'

'You've got a nerve,' she hissed at him.

'Yes,' he agreed. 'And you're a reporter?'

'You're darned well right I'm a reporter,' she snapped. And then was struck by her father's admonition. A good reporter tries to get the facts right, but the biggest problem is to spell all the names right! 'What's——' she stammered. 'I—I have to know for my story, what your name is?'

His grin spread farther. Ear to ear? That's impossible, she thought. But nice! Why does *that* word keep intruding on things?

'Clarke,' he said. 'James Francis Clarke. With an *e* on the end. Civil Engineer. My friends call me Jim.'

'I'll bet they do,' she snapped, ignoring the invitation to tell him who she was. Her eyes were scanning the floor for her lost notebook. He moved one rather large foot, and revealed it. She dropped gracefully to bended knees and retrieved it. 'What do you Civil Engineer?'

'Bridges,' he laughed. 'Is this an exclusive interview?'

'Yes—No——' No way do I want to get involved with this man, one to one, she told herself. But the Devil drove. Her editor would not accept excuses—just stories. And here was a possible source, if handled right. Unfortunately he seemed to be reading her mind.

'Your editor will be pretty mad at you for coming in late,' he offered. 'Maybe I could fill you in on some of the details?'

'Well——' she admitted grouchily, 'well—perhaps you could.'

'Over lunch,' he added.

She took a quick look at her digital wristwatch. Twelve o'clock noon. Vicky would be home at two-fifteen. The party was scheduled for three. Should I let this heaven-sent chance escape?

'There's no restaurant in the city that will let that— that dog of yours in,' she sighed. 'Share a sandwich?'

'Anything,' he returned. 'My dog likes hamburger for lunch. How about you?'

Twenty minutes later, squeezed together in her little Fiat, with the dog occupying the whole of the back seat, she drove them over the old bridge to the island in the middle of the river, and out on to the flat lip of Marine Park. It's several acres of land, some of it reclaimed from the sea, sported a grassed picnic area, children's slides, and a clear view of both the lower and upper harbour.

They climbed out of the little car and he watched as she spread a blanket over the bonnet of the vehicle, and set out the McDonald's take-away cartons. Above their heads, malicious seagulls made military dive-bombing inspections, but sheered off when the dog mustered up a deep resonant bark.

'How in the world do you tell which end to feed?' she inquired, looking at the màss of fur.

'Easy. You feed the end that doesn't wag. So alright, she could use a trim, or something. I just never seem to have the time. What is this place?'

'It's called Marine Park,' she told him. 'I thought you were a bridge expert?'

'I am.' There was a smile tangled into the words as he looked around. 'Bridges in general, not this one specifically. I don't suppose that thing over there is the bridge everyone is complaining about?'

'You've never seen it?' She gasped. 'How——'

'Hey,' he cautioned. 'This State has four-hundred-and-eighty-five bridges, mostly falling down. And the ones over navigable waterways belong to the Army Corps of Engineers. No I've never seen it before. Tell me about it?'

Somehow or another, she knew, the world was working upside down. She had come to hear the expert, and he was asking her to explain the problem to him. Talk about the blind leading the blind! If Dad were here, he'd die laughing, and then file one whale of a story. The very thought of her big capable father gave her enough of a boost to take on the project.

'The harbour is about a mile wide at this spot,' she lectured. 'The city of New Bedford lies on those hills to the west. The town of Fairhaven is on the flatland to the east. The old main highway, Route Six, goes over the bridge, through both towns. There are two islands in a row, here. Fish Island is close to the New Bedford shore. Between Fish Island and Pope Island, where we're standing, there is a deepwater channel. And that lovely old lady over there is a swing bridge over the channel. Now, after you get over the bridge, there's a causeway that connects Pope Island to the Fairhaven shore. Small boats can get into the upper harbour by going under the causeway. Bigger boats —commercial craft—have to go through the channel. And for that they have to swing the bridge to one side. Only the bridge keeps getting stuck, either open or closed. If it sticks in the open position, people have to drive up-river to the next bridge, and, of course, all these businesses on the island lose a lot of money. If it gets stuck in the closed position, then none of the fishing fleet can go up-river to the fish processing plants. And fishing is our lifeblood here, on both sides of the river.'

'Very neat summary,' he chuckled. 'Go to the head of the class. But it doesn't seem to be all that much of a problem. What's that, upstream?' He gestured into the distance, where two other man-made spans crossed the bay at a much narrower point.'

'They're about a mile away,' she acknowledged. 'The nearest one is the new super-highway bridge. It's sort of non-stop, so to speak. It goes around both New Bedford and Fairhaven. And the one behind it is an old causeway. But the streets in New Bedford and Fairhaven are so small and crowded at each end of the causeway that it makes for a tough traffic problem.'

'So it's an annoyance when the old bridge sticks?' Go ahead and laugh, wise guy, she stormed silently at him. Go ahead and laugh. You just try living around here sometime, and you'd learn.

'Yes,' she responded through stiffened lips. 'Very annoying. It's been sticking for the last umpteen years!'

She turned away from him, into the wind, which was whistling up the channel from the southeast. Although the sun was bright in the September air, it was cool standing on the exposed island. It was a perky sort of wind, that tinkered for a moment with her loose braids, then solved the knots and blew her long silken hair out behind her. At her feet it treated his dog the same way, blowing back the long hair from its face, exposing a curiously stubbed nose, and sparkling, intelligent eyes. The dog panted, grinning at her, with its heavy tail pounding the turf. Like dog, like master she told herself. They're both—grinning at me. If this was a cannibal island I would begin to worry what the main dish was going to be!

'And what's that thing down there?' He had moved up beside her, dropping one muscular arm over her shoulder and pulling her closer to him. She looked at her left shoulder, where his hand rested. Put him in his place? Say something caustic? Unhand me, you villain? Oh Lord, why bother. Her eyes traced his pointing finger.

'That's the hurricane barrier,' she told him. A good mile down the harbour a huge barrage of piled rocks cut off the harbour itself from the outer bay. A pair of massive steel gates stood open in its middle. 'We've had two or three hurricanes come up the coastline and raise havoc in the lowlands along the river here. So they built a barrier. It certainly works. There hasn't been a hurricane up here since. You can see how low the land is, all the way up the river. And those brick buildings, the old cotton mills? The mills themselves have long since gone south, but the buildings are occupied by a variety of manufacturing firms now.'

'Solve a problem, make a problem,' he commented.

'What?'

'An old engineering principle. Make sure your solution to the present problem doesn't create a bigger problem.' His hand squeezed her gently to emphasise what he was saying.

'I don't understand.'

'Bet you a nickel,' he said. 'You can't mock the sea, and if you shut it out, you pay for it. Right now I'll wager that there is a sand bar gradually building up against the outside of that wall. In another thirty to fifty years it will be so solid that the channel will require dredging. Give it another fifty years after that, and this harbour will be an inland lake. Bet?'

'No,' she laughed. 'What a cynic you are! I won't bet. People like you are always right. Vicky can worry about it, but not me.'

'Vicky?'

'I-a little girl I know,' she stammered. Damn! How did that sneak into the conversation. He seems to—he's put a coat of oil on my tongue! She shrugged her shoulders, and pulled her cardigan closer. 'I have to go now, Mr Clarke. I——'

'I understand. You don't have to explain to me about dead-lines and things like that. Do you have to drive all the way back to Providence to file your story?'

'I-dear me, no. I-I just telephone it in, you know.'

'Oh?'

You can wait as long as you want to, she told him under her breath, and you're not going to get another word on that out of me. Not a word. He was watching her closely, eyes glued to hers. The silence lay over them like a blanket, until finally punctured by the hoarse whistle of a small freighter calling for the bridge to be opened.

'Okay,' he laughed. 'I can take a hint. Could you perhaps drive me to one of the hotels in the city?'

'No, I'm afraid not,' she said solemnly. 'We don't have any hotels in this area. There's a motel though, just across the bridge in Fairhaven. It's on my way home. Want me to drop you off?'

'That would be a help. I'll need to rent a car. Prichard and I came down together in a State vehicle, and he took that back with him. I should have thought . . . Do you suppose this motel would object to my dog?'

'You'd better believe it would.'

'And you don't intend to offer any suggestions?'

'It's not my dog,' she muttered. At which the animal struggled to its feet and looked mournfully at her. Fully extended, standing squarely on its own four legs, it came up to her upper thigh. And the mournful look— that came all the way up to her heart. Sucker, she lectured herself sternly. Don't we have enough clutter at home already?

'It would only have to be for a day or two,' he prodded. She looked at him out of the corner of her eye. The grin was firmly in place. What a con man he is, she thought. He can actually make those eyes twinkle. Damn! And he knows he's won already. Why am I so obvious to everybody? Lord, I wish my father were home.

'As it happens, Mr Clarke,' she said, doing her best to maintain that outward poise any experienced reporter would have, 'I live on a farm. My grandfather's farm. It's about twelve miles from here, in the town of Rochester. I suppose—your dog is housetrained?'

'Her? Perfect manners, ma'am. Never a doubt.

There's only one small problem. She think's that she's human, and she tends to get lonely in the night. No real problem, of course. And now that we're going to be friends, you haven't told me your name.'

'It's Clark,' she giggled. 'Like yours, but without the *e* at the end. Samantha Clark.'

'How convenient,' he said softly, accepting her proffered hand. 'How very convenient. Married? Engaged?'

'Perhaps.' It was a struggle, getting her hand back. *His* hand did not appear to be pressing, but she just could not get her hand back. And it was important. Touching him like this was—disturbing!

'My hand, please,' she insisted. 'It's the one I write with.'

'Oh! I was thinking about something.'

'You don't need my hand for that,' she snapped. He smiled as he released her. 'If you want me to, I'll take your dog with me—but only for a couple of days, you understand. I—oh my, look at the time. I have to get home.'

She dropped him off at the Bridge Motel. There were only a few cars in the parking area, so she knew he could easily get a room.

'I'm in the 'phone book,' she told him as he climbed out. 'It's in Grandpa's name. Clark. You could remember that? Ephraim Clark. You can't miss it.'

He waved as she shifted the ancient car into gear and pulled out on to Route Six. From the back seat his dog, recognising a parting, began to moan softly. It continued throughout the whole trip until they finally passed Haskell Swamp on Mattapoiset Road, and turned up the gravel road that led to the house. She sat and looked for just a moment. The old farmhouse, built before the end of the 19th century, showed a red-brick centre, two stories high, and two single-storied wooden wings, added haphazardly at a later date. It was not a thing of beauty, but it was all the home her much-travelled family had. She moved the car up between the house and the barn, and opened the door to let the animal out.

'Mommy!' The little high-pitched voice was attached to a squirming, squirreling little girl, who ran into her arms as soon as she was out of the car. 'I beat you home! You should see what good work I done at school. I got a star in reading, and a star in arithmetic. Ain't that wonderful!'

'Wonderful!' Samantha laughed down at the towhead buried in her skirt. She could feel the burst of love that contact made, deep abiding love for this orphaned niece of hers, left in her care by the whim of an airplane accident five years before. Samantha bent over and traded kisses. At almost eight, Vicky was already more of a load than Sam cared to pick up, except in emergencies. The dog took that moment to stick her head around the front of the car and beg introduction.

'It's a dog?' The girl was astonished. 'It's almost big enough to ride. I'll bet my old saddle would fit him— her?'

'I'm not sure,' Samantha chuckled. 'There's too much hair to tell at the moment. I suppose another sheep dog could tell right away. We'll call it It.'

They walked over to the house, Vicky in the middle, with one arm around Samantha's waist, the other resting on the dog's head. The screen door was in place, the wooden door behind it open.

'Mother?' Samantha called as they went up the stairs. Through the screen door she could hear the squeak of the wheelchair. They went in single-file, with Vicky in the lead.

Samantha exchanged a secret smile with her beautiful mother. A tall, willowy blonde, sprinkled with spots of white now, her smooth skin furrowed with pain-furrow originating in the accident that had left her unable to walk. 'What in the world is that?'

That walked over to the wheelchair and stared. The dog was first to break the stalemate. It's big tongue came out and licked the hand resting on the wheel of the chair.

'Samantha?'

'Yes, I know.' She looked down at her mother with a half-innocent smile on her face. 'But he—the man, not the dog—was in a bind. Its not exactly a stray, or anything . . .'

'Your grandfather will have something to say about that! Can you be sure this—this animal can get along with the farm dogs?'

'But Grandfather won't be home for another week,' Samantha sighed. 'The dog is only going to be here for a few days at most. Two or three, perhaps.'

'And there's a man attached?'

'Yes. I—he was at the briefing, and he was going to some hotel, but of course there aren't any, and they wouldn't—at the Motel, I mean—they wouldn't take the dog, and I—oh Mom, have I made a mess, as usual?'

'No of course you haven't.' The warmth of love lightened the distance between them. Samantha leaned over to share a hug, to kiss the soft cheek. It would be so good to stay like this, she told herself. Cradled in warmth and appreciation. I need to be loved!

'You gotta get the stuff, Mom,' the child interrupted. 'It's only half-an-hour, and you ain't got cookies or nothing for the party.'

'Hey, don't talk like that,' Samantha returned. 'What do you suppose I was doing last night while you were sleeping? Come on now. I need everybody's help to get set up. Everybody into the kitchen!'

'That's my line,' her mother laughed. 'Bright-eyed and bushy tailed, everyone into the kitchen. Remember, Sam?'

How could I forget, Samantha sighed as she followed the procession into the big farm kitchen. The two sisters, Kate and Sam it had been in those days. Big Kate, ten years the senior, and little Sam. Kate, who had married so happily, and was so cherished. She had come over from her home in Swansea, where her husband George owned a store in the mall, and arranged to leave two-year-old Vicky at the farmhouse while the two of them

went off on their long-postponed honeymoon.
Everything had been laughter. After lunch they refused
transportation to the airport. They intended to do it all
themselves, Kate had laughed. And so that was it.
Kisses all around, a cheer as their car spun its wheels in
the gravel, and that was it. Nothing more, ever.

Somewhere over Corfu their jetliner had plunged into
the sea, and no bodies were ever recovered. That was
the memory. They just walked out the door and
disappeared. How do you explain that to a two-year-
old child? Or a weeping mother, for that matter? Or to
a tiny sister who loved them so very much?

It had changed everything. Mother was unable to
cope with a growing baby. Father was constantly away
in his job as a war correspondent, and Grandfather had
the farm to run. So Samantha Clark had given up her
dream of a university and a journalistic career, to stay
home and keep the family going.

'Do you regret it?' her grandfather had asked once,
after a busy night with a fear-haunted child.

'No. Not a minute,' she had told him. And meant
every word of it. There were compensations in the heart
that the world could never see.

By three-thirty that afternoon the birthday party was
in full swing. Nine children of Vicky's age and younger
had come. And following the country custom, at least
one parent of each child had stayed to help with the
work. The cookies were soon gone, along with eight
gallons of ice cream, three pitchers of punch, and all of
a magnificent cake. A few knees required mending, two
disagreements required arbitration, and clouds were
banking in the western twilight as the various cars were
loaded up. As the last one drove off, Samantha and
Vicky waved goodbye from the gate. The little girl
moved close to Sam and put both hands around her
waist.

'It was the nicest party ever, and you're the nicest
mother I ever had,' she said. 'I think I'll love you
forever and ever!'

'Yes, or until the nicest boy in the world comes

along,' Samantha laughed. 'But don't make it sound so aging. It makes people look for my glasses and cane.'

'Mommy?' The little girl was standing on one leg, scratching at the other, concentrating on something. 'Did I ever have another Mommy? Sometimes—I seem to remember somebody. Very big. Not short, like you. Did I?'

Oh Lord, Samantha thought, not now. It's been a long tiring day. Not now. But the psychiatrist had said, 'As soon as she brings up the subject, but not before.' The picture was still vivid. Vicky, just four years old, drooping around the house, always searching in corners, always afraid of visitors. And then one early morning, trailing her favourite teddy bear by its mangled hind leg, she had stumbled into Samantha's room with a big smile on her face.

'I know now,' she had chortled. 'It was a secret, wasn't it! *You're* my Mommy. Aren't you? Aren't you Sam?'

Not knowing what to say, Samantha had sat up in her bed and extended her arms in welcome. And from that moment on she had been Vicky's mother. And now it was accounting time?

'Yes,' she said softly. 'Once you had another mother. My sister Kate. And a daddy, too. They were lovely people.'

'And did they just go away and leave me? Sara Pincton said that at school. Her mother said it. Did they?'

'No, love. They didn't just go away and leave you. God called them Home. He had something else he needed them to do. You do understand?'

The little girl pondered, and then squeezed Samantha's hand. 'Of course,' she said sturdily. 'I ain't no baby. I'm eight years old today. God called them Home. Well, after all, I got you, don't I?'

'Yes, you've got me, baby.' And don't press any more facts on her than she needs, the psychiatrist had said. 'Anything else?'

'Well—just—Sam, you oughta get married. You're

pretty and nice and everything. And then I could have a father too.'

'Why you sweet little bird. There's always Charlie, isn't there? You do like him, don't you?'

'Well—he's not very big, Mommy, and he always seems to be around the house, isn't he?'

'It's supposed to be that way, love. Charlie and I have know each other since we were in Middle School. I guess you might say that we're going steady. Walking out, they say.'

'He's better than nothing, Mom. Go ahead and marry him.'

'Thank you Miss Muffet. And now there's supper to make.' She took the little girl and pointed her toward the house, giving her a pat on her bottom for starters. It might have worked, but there was a distraction.

A car came smoothly up the road. Slowly, as if the driver were looking for an unfamiliar address. And then more quickly, as if he had found it. It was a sleek little Corvette, replete with spoilers and racing lines And the driver!

'Who is it, Sam,' the little girl asked. 'Not the milkman?'

'No, love. Certainly not the milkman. He is the man who owns the dog.'

'I had a hard time finding this place,' he commented as he vaulted out of the car. Look at that, Samantha told herself. The wolf, out looking for Red Riding Hood. Or somebody. Don't I have enough troubles on my hands already? Look at that big smile. I wish *I* had a dimple. What a con artist. Turn him off, Samantha, there's a good girl!

'Well, I told you it was a farm,' she returned coolly. 'You didn't think it would be in downtown New Bedford, did you?'

'Introduce me!' Vicky was tugging at her skirt, impatient to know.

'Ah—yes. Mr Clarke, may I present Miss Clark?'

'We got the same name?' Vicky glowed, working on some secret dream of her own.

Just what in the world is he doing here, Samantha wondered to herself. All that way to come, and it *is* difficult to find if you are a stranger. Why? Just to see his dog? Look at those curls! Damn the man. Why does he bother me so? 'Please, Vicky,' she snapped, 'don't be a pest.' And immediately she had regrets. 'I'm sorry, baby,' she added with more warmth. 'I-I guess I'm tired.'

'I did want to see how the dog was adapting to the country air,' he said jauntily. 'She's a city dog, I'm afraid. Without all the traffic noises she could get lonesome.'

Woman and girl exchanged knowing looks. At least that settles one small problem, Samantha chuckled to herself. He came to see his dog. 'She's adapting, Mr Clarke. In fact, she's out back cleaning up after the birthday party.'

'Birthday party?' He walked in through the gate without waiting for an invitation, and moved up towards the house. Compelled, the two followed along after him. 'I hate to miss a birthday party,' he continued. 'Yours, Samantha? Twenty-one?'

'Boy, you sure don't know nothin',' Vicky answered. 'It was my birthday. I used to be seven. Now I'm eight. And Sam, she's a lot older than me.'

'Yes, I could see that,' he returned. Samantha could see the laugh-devils flashing in his blue eyes. Noxious male, she told herself. Altogether too sure of himself by a long shot.

'Is that what you call her—Sam?' For the first time she noticed the smooth baritone voice.

'Who me?' Vicky squeaked. 'I call her lots of things, like Sam, yes. But you'd better not. She don't like no men callin' her Sam. Only me. Not even Grandpa, or Great Grandpa. So you better be careful.'

'Yes, I can see that,' he answered the child solemnly. 'I'll be very careful not to call her Sam. She doesn't *look* like a Sam to me, anyway. What else do you call her if she doesn't like Sam?'

The girl cocked her head, trying to judge him. 'Well,

it's hard to say. Sometimes I call her Merry Sunshine. That's what her daddy calls her. But most of the time I call her Mom. Not you, though. You can't call her Mom.'

'No,' he answered. There was a stress in his voice, a nuance that Samantha caught but did not understand. He stopped, turned, and stared at them both. 'Pretty as a picture,' he said. 'Same hair, same face, same eyes. Beautiful. No, I won't call her Mom. Not ever. And now . . .' he shook his head, as if trying to clear some cobwebs. 'And now, Mrs Clark, if I could see my dog?'

'Miss Clark.' It was an automatic correction, the sort of thing one does without thinking. She gave him a quick smile and led him around the corner of the house, to where his dog was up to her long sticky earlobes in left-over ice cream and cookies. The animal completely ignored his arrival.

'Will you look at that,' he muttered. 'I'll have to put her on a diet. She's already twenty-six pounds overweight.'

'Do you want me to stop her?' Samantha was unable to explain to herself why she felt so anxious about the matter, but she did.

'No, don't bother,' he returned. 'Let her have her last days' fun. I'll be by to pick her up in the morning.'

'Oh? I thought you were going to leave her for several days.'

'I changed my mind. I'm going to look up a good kennel for her for the rest of the month.'

'Oh.' What a great conversationalist I'm getting to be, she told herself. Two hundred basic English words. Why would he want to take her to a kennel? He was perfectly satisfied before with the idea of leaving her on the farm. Have we said something wrong?

'I'd better be going, *Miss* Clark.' You could almost hear him underlining the word.

'You won't stay to dinner? You haven't met my mother——'

'No. I do have to be going. You're not married?'

'No, I——'

'I see. Divorced?'

'No. I never have been——'

'Yes, well, I do have to run. See you tomorrow.'

His dog continued to ignore him, her nose rooted deep in the last of the paper ice cream containers. He stood for a moment, hand half-raised towards the dog, and then he did it.

Run, that is. Or at least so it seemed to the other two. They straggled along behind him down to his car, but he was already inside, motor warming, when they arrived. Dirt spewed from under the black wheels as he made a racing U-turn, and was quickly out of sight.

'Wow!' Vicky contributed.

'Wow indeed,' Samantha returned. Her thumbnail flicked at her lower lip in a long-established habit. 'I didn't expect him to come, but I did think he would stay longer, baby.'

'Maybe he don't like little girls?'

'Why would you say that?'

'He was all smiles till we got up to the house, that's all. Gee, he'd be great for it.'

'Great for what, baby?'

'You wouldn't understand, Mom.' Samantha noted that secretive smile on the little girl's face. She ran a finger through the child's blowing hair, and walked back to the house with her, arm in arm.

'Who was that?' Her mother was at the door, waiting. 'I heard the voices and thought to come out, but he was gone before I could make it.'

'Oh, it was just——'

'It was the dog man, Grandma. He likes Sam. You could tell.'

'You should have invited him for dinner,' her mother said. 'We could always stretch the clam chowder.'

'Yes, I know,' she returned, not willing to continue the debate. 'I have to call in my story.'

The pair of them separated to let Sam through. The *Gazette* was a major morning paper in Southern New England, and each stringer had a specific time in which to call in on assigned stories. Although Samantha had only been on the part-time job for three months, she realised the importance of timing.

It took her a minute to rearrange her notes in front of her. Stringers don't write stories. They just deliver facts. When the cheery voice answered, '*The Gazette*,' she said quickly, 'Re-write please.' A click, a ring, a moment of waiting, and then a raspy familiar voice.

'Re-write. Donohue.'

'Samantha Clark. The press conference in New Bedford about the new Fairhaven bridge.'

'Shoot.'

Steadily she read him the facts, and stopped talking. 'That's all?'

'Yes,' she said hesitantly, then, 'Mr Donohue, would you tell the editor that I was late for the conference? The bridge was stuck open for an hour and ten minutes when I drove in.'

A short silence, and then a burst of laughter. 'He won't mind, girl. Not after he reads this.'

'He won't mind?'

'Not a bit. Gotta go.' And he did.

What in the world does all *that* mean, she asked herself. In a world where stories were sacred, being late was almost the death knell of a career. 'He won't mind?' What a funny thing to say. The day seemed filled with people saying things she just did not understand. Like Mr Clarke, for example.

And then her very brilliant mind began lining up snatches of conversation. Vicky: 'I call her Mom.' Me: 'No, I'm not married.' Me: 'No, I'm not divorced. I've never been married.' Good gracious Lord! Wow! What in the world can he be thinking of me?

Somewhat bemused, she wandered out to the kitchen, where her mother was struggling to baste a chicken which had long since outlived its usefulness. 'Maybe I should have stewed it,' her mother suggested apologetically.

'No, I don't think so. It's been on a slow roast for long enough. We'll be able to eat it—I think. Thank the Lord, Grandfather's not home.'

'What did you say his name was?' Her mother was probing to a purpose, but Sam was daydreaming as she used the plastic syringe. Why was it of any importance what he thought of her? But it was. She knew it was.

'His name is Clarke,' Vicky answered for her. 'Just like us—Clarke.'

'No, not quite,' Samantha added hastily. 'He has an *e* on the end. Clarke with an *e*.'

'How nice,' her mother said, hugely satisfied.

'Nice,' Vicky repeated. 'Real nice. Just what we need.'

Samantha continued basting the bird, totally oblivious of the atmosphere around her. And when Charlie came by that night for their weekly movie-date, she told him all about it, and was surprised by his dour reaction.

CHAPTER TWO

SAMANTHA woke up automatically at six o'clock. Chickens laid eggs seven days a week, and the household ate them. Which, according to Grandpa's standards, made feeding them woman's work. She fumbled for her old green robe, stumbling over the dog as she did so. 'Monster!' The animal failed to move a muscle. It had been a terrible night.

It started off well enough. The chicken turned out to be edible, though just barely. The movie was a period swashbuckler, of the type that tickled Sam madly, and the whole house had settled down. Until midnight.

The wind came up at about that time. A raucous gusty wind that rocked the old house, and set it creaking. And then the dog started to complain. Not a worthwhile honest bark. Not even a challenging bay. Not this dog. Left on the back porch for the night, she had begun to scratch at the door, emitting a pained whine that rattled the nerves. So downstairs Samantha had traipsed, to drag the monster into the kitchen, where a rug was provided. And so back to bed.

At two o'clock the wind rose again, and so did the complaints. Until finally, in a high state of disgust, Samantha had dragged the animal up the stairs, pushed it into a comfortable ball on her bedroom rug, and threatened its very life. After which they both slept.

When her alarm went off at six-ten, she had accumulated enough clothing for the morning, and was about to play blind man's bluff with the stairs. The dog was too tired to move, and remained camped out on the rug.

'I'll get you, dog,' Samantha threatened as she backed out into the hall. 'One of these days. You watch. You and that crazy man who owns you. You watch and see if I don't.' The animal half-opened one lazy eye, and promptly went back to sleep.

And so down to her mother, to help her into her chair, then to the kitchen, to set out the cereal breakfast for Vicky, and to organise a dish of scrambled eggs for her mother. Mrs Clark came along the hall at six-thirty, as usual. Since the accident, the downstairs sitting room had been turned into a bedroom for her, to allow maximum comfort. She could do *most* things for herself, and insisted on it. While she wheeled her chair up to the old kitchen table, and sipped at her first cup of coffee, Samantha moved ahead to pack a school lunch. And then, after a quick trip upstairs to make sure that Vicky was really getting out of bed, it was out to the chicken-run, to scatter cracked grain, check the water, and pick up the day's supply of eggs.

At eight o'clock the little girl was down at the road by the mail box, waiting for the school bus. Mrs Clark was bathed, dressed, and ensconced on the porch for her morning air. And when Samantha dropped into a chair for just a moment's rest after such a long morning, the grandfather clock in the hall startled her by announcing that it was only eight-fifteen!

Look at me, Samantha lectured herself. Scrubby denims, a blouse with two tears in the collar and a button missing. My hair is a mess. I'm worn out, and its only eight in the morning. Whatever happened to that millionaire who was going to come along and snatch me up into *happy ever after*? So much for childish dreams. Up, girl. Up, up and away!

With a little smile playing at the corners of her mouth, she drove herself up the stairs, made the beds, and then settled down in front of her typewriter. Bread and butter money. Charlie Aikens, a young farmer, *the boy next door* for all of Samantha's young life, was also a part-time insurance adjustor. Twice a week he dropped off typing work, and paid a reasonable sum for it, along with a few surreptitious hugs and kisses.

'Samantha! Telephone for you. Your editor!'

She finished the line she was working on, flexed her

fingers, and wearily pushed her chair back. My editor! What a laugh. Her mother seemed to equate every voice that called from the *Gazette* to be that of the editor. As if J. Edward Bainsboro ever took time to speak to a mere stringer. But if it was the Assignments desk, it might be a nice little story. Which translated into 'found' money. And every bit was added to the family fund. And some day! She dropped a kiss on the top of her mother's head in passing, and picked up the telephone.

'Samantha Clark here.' She was doing her best to cultivate an impersonal business-like voice on the telephone, but most of the time her husky contralto cracked at the wrong times.

'Samantha? Bainsboro here.'

'Sure it is,' she chuckled. 'Come on now, I know better than that. Who is this? Donohue?'

'Young lady!' The voice had a snap to it, and not a little impatience. 'This happens to be J. Edward Bainsboro.'

'I—for real? I—well . . .' and as usual under pressure, her brain blew up and lost control. Babble, babble babble. Lord, help me shut my mouth quickly. 'Isn't it a lovely day, Mr Bainsboro?'

'It happens to be raining like hell in Providence,' he rasped. 'Look, Samantha. I'm sorry I didn't have time to talk to you when you first came aboard. I should have known you would be your father's daughter. Great story that, about the bridge. A lot of good humour. And I do love a reporter who sticks the knife in politicians. Look. I want a couple of follow-up stories about the bridge. In the same vein, mind you. Lay it on good. Maybe you could get that engineer fellow to talk to you again, hey? Make it a full column. There'll be a bonus cheque for that last one.' Bang.

Samantha stood still for an endless moment, the receiver still at her ear. Good story? Bonus? Get that engineer fellow to say something more? Bang! He hung up before I could even get a word in edgewise. What story? If it was good, all the credit belongs to Re-write.

I wonder how it came out. I suppose I'll just have to wait.

The *Gazette* was a morning paper, but along the Rural Free Delivery Routes, it would arrive either late in the afternoon, or more likely, the next day.

'Trouble, dear?' Her mother had wheeled herself in from the kitchen, where she had been peeling onions. There were onion-tears in her eyes.

'No, not really. That really *was* the editor, Mom. He might speak to famous reporters, like Dad, but not to people like me! You really shouldn't try to peel onions, love. You do too much work around here as it is. The doctor said you were to rest.'

'I *am* resting,' her mother returned. 'It does a girl good to have a real cry once and again. And I'm not about to sit in a corner and turn to ashes, Samantha Clark. I intend to keep doing. Now, what did Mr High-and-Mighty have to say?'

'What did he say?' Her eyes sparkled, turning her commonplace face into a thing of amazing animation. 'He said . . .' and here she did a plausible imitation of the editor's raspy tones 'that was a fine story you did on the bridge. There'll be a bonus. Get us another story from that young fellow.'

'Oh Sam! You've turned the corner!'

'Well if I did, I didn't see it. All I did was talk to the Re-write desk Mom, the same as always. I think he must have me mixed up with some other Clark.'

'Don't be foolish, dear. There just can't be another Samantha Clark in New England. That's wonderful. And now if you could only hear about your book.'

'Oh yeah, sure I'll hear about it.' Samantha shrugged her shoulders. Her great opus. Five rejections so far. And it ought to come bouncing home again any day now. Like a homing pigeon, no less. Still talking to her mother, Sam backed away from her, *en route* to her typing desk upstairs, when she felt herself run into something that reached just to hip level, and fell over it, backwards, landing with a crack on the bare floor. As she half-sat there, her legs still balancing over the back of—of course—that DAMN DOG again! It's hard not to think of her in capital letters, she told herself, as she leaned over on one side and used a hand to explore the damage.

'Sam? Sam! Did you hurt yourself?'

'No, only my pride, Mother. But you, dog. What have you to say for yourself?'

One end of the animal turned in her direction, and a long rough tongue came out and began to lick her nose.'

'You don't escape it that easy, you rascal!' Sam used both hands to frame the dog's head, brushing back the fringe of hair that almost completely concealed the face. The big eyes looked at her dolefully. It was too much for her sense of humour. The giggles ran the scale of delight. The dog's big mouth opened and panted at her. It moved forward two steps, sat, and began it's ministrations again.

'Alright already,' she gasped, struggling to her feet. 'You poor dear. I'll bet you can't see where you're going at all. You need to be clipped, or whatever they do. Right?' The dog responded with a dignified *whoof* and stretched out on the floor.

'Not now, idiot. You've had a good night's sleep. Out. Outside. Do whatever it is that your kind of dog does. Out!'

Lordy, Samantha thought, looking out at the cloudless sky. It's raining in Providence, fifty miles away. It won't be long before it gets here. Back to work, girl! But she had barely managed to get another two forms completed when some madman began pounding on the front door, rattling the panels, stabbing at the bell.

Another one of those days, she sighed. And Charlie will be here tonight to pick up this work—if I ever get it finished. Well, Mother knows I'm working, and she'll get the door, and——

'Samantha! Samantha! There's a young man here to see you.'

'I'm working, Mom,' she called back. 'Tell him we don't want any. Tell him to come back next week or something. Tell him . . .'

She could hear the stomp of heavy feet on the stairs. Angry feet. You get that sort of feeling about feet coming up the stairs. Happy feet, scared feet, angry feet. And this pair was definitely angry!

When he came through her open door her guess was confirmed. Angry. Lord, boiling angry. James Clarke, Civil Engineer. Look at the way those curls are bouncing. Even they look angry! Sam pushed back and slid her chair away from the typewriter.

'Really, Mr Clarke,' she stammered. 'I'm not in the practice of entertaining men in my bedroom. Whatever in the world do you think you're doing?'

He stomped over to her, so close that she stood up and backed away, until her knees hit against the bed. 'Really, Miss Clark!' He was doing his best to mimic her tone. 'How do I know who you entertain in your bedroom. Look at me!'

Samantha was finding it almost impossible not to do so. His face was red. There was a little tic going at the corner of his mouth. Oh Lordy. She did her best to shrink into invisibility. His hands dropped on to her shoulders. She could feel the individual fingers as they pressed into her soft flesh. One shake. My head's going to come off, she screamed at herself.

'This morning I got up filled with the milk of human kindness,' he roared at her. 'I thought about you all night long. Did you know that?'

'I—no,' she managed to squeak out.

'I told myself that it didn't matter what you used to be. Not to me. I told myself, Jim, I said, that's one hell of a girl. That's what I said. You hear me?'

'I—yes. I—one hell of a girl—yes!'

'And then I said, Jim, you get your backside out there, and you tell her just that, see, and you see if you can do something about it. You hear?'

'I—It's hard not to. Please don't yell at me, Mr Clarke.' From some hidden depth Samantha had found a reserve of courage. Just enough to answer back one time. No more.

'Yell at you?' he roared. 'Wait'll I get warmed up. Then I'll yell at you, lady!'

'Samantha? Are you alright, Samantha?' Her mother's voice from the bottom of the stairs, was just the impulse she needed to fire up her own volatile temper. 'Just who the devil do you think you are, storming into my house, breaking into my bedroom, roaring at me like—like some demented giant! And get your hands off me, you—you . . .'

Whatever it was she was about to call him failed to make it up to the mark. He returned her glare, but somehow or another his face kept getting closer and closer, blotting out the light. Sam squeaked in alarm, and then his lips crossed hers and shut off all her senses. Very suddenly, the world seemed to have disappeared. All she could feel or sense was the moist warmth of him as his lips pressed urgently against hers. For a half-second she struggled. And then her defences crumbled. Her lips softened under his probing. Her mindless body crowded against him, fitting all her soft contours into his rock-hard muscles, shivering, whimpering. Until he forced her away, holding her at arms length. Holding her up, for that matter, because her shivering legs were failing in their primary function.

'That's what I was going to do,' he gruffed. 'Tell your mother you're alright.'

'I—I'm alright, Mother,' she called. The words came meekly through trembling lips. She felt the mad urge to crowd up against him again, but his strength held her off. 'But now you're not going to do that?' she whispered.

'No. I'm not going to do that,' he snapped. His hands discharged her. She collapsed on the edge of the bed. She sat there quietly, waiting. Her hands fumbled with each other, and finally settled, clasped, in her lap.

'But you did,' she muttered, glaring up at him. 'Why?'

'That was just to show you what you're missing,' he snapped. 'Did you write this garbage?' He brandished a well-thumbed newspaper in front of her. She re-focused her eyes. He was waving the second section of the *Gazette* in front of her.

Rhode Island is the smallest state in the Union. And its capital, Providence, is squeezed hard up against the southern border of Massachusetts. So the *Gazette*, the major metropolitan newspaper in the region, published a daily second section marked Massachusetts News. Sam reached for the paper and brought it down to eye-level. The headline read, *The Bridge of Sighs?* And under it was an old file photo of the bridge.

'My glasses,' she begged. 'I can't read without my glasses. On the typing table?' He complied. She slipped them on, glad to have the protection of their very utilitarian horn rims. And then she gasped. The story beneath the photo was not the typical short snappy story that the Re-write desk would ordinarily grind out. Instead it was almost word for word, her exact report, just as she had given it on the telephone. The first paragraph recalled the problems of the bridge. The second described the model of the proposed new bridge. And then,

'The principal speaker was Mr John Prichard, former representative from the Tenth District, who lost his seat in the last election, and was appointed Commissioner of Public Works by his friends, to keep him off the Welfare rolls. Mr Prichard said that the new bridge would be finished in three years. His companion, Mr James Clarke, a Civil Engineer, said it would take seven years. I asked Mr Prichard what we would use to get across the river in the meantime. He said that the old bridge was perfectly fine, and would serve us well. I was late for the briefing, so I thought I might get something from Mr Clarke, who appears to be a nice young man. I bought him a hamburger at McDonalds, but he said he didn't know anything about the bridge, since he had never seen it before. By the way, I was late for the briefing because the bridge was stuck in the open position for an hour and a half.'

And then, underneath the story, in script type, a note

purporting to be from the editor.

'Buying a hamburger for a civil servant, Samantha, is bribery. Bot don't worry. The *Gazette* will provide you a lawyer. Put both hamburgers on the expense account.'

J.E.B.

'Well,' he commented.

'I—well what?'

'Did you write that?'

'I—well—yes, I wrote it. So what?'

'So what? You make me appear to be a damn fool in print, and you say *so what*?'

'I—please. Don't yell at me any more. My eyes are weak, but my ears work just fine! Did I write something that was untrue?'

'Oh no!' His sarcasm was so thick you could spread it with a knife. 'Oh no! He's a nice young engineer, doesn't know a thing about the bridge! Smart aleck!'

'I—well—what part is it that's wrong? You're not a nice young engineer? Or you don't know anything about the bridge?'

'Both,' he roared back at her. 'Neither. Oh hell, what's the use talking to somebody like you. Where's my dog?'

'I—can I get up now?'

He looked down at her, puzzled. 'Get up? Who's stopping you from getting up?'

'It—you—there's no room, with you standing like that. You have to move back a way, and——'

'Okay, okay. I get the message. He backed off a couple of paces. She stood up warily.

'I was right,' he said, staring at her head. Her plaits had both burst loose, tumbling her long silky hair down around her shoulders, providing a reflected halo around her heart-shaped face. 'By God, I was right.'

'Look, Mr Clarke,' she snapped at him. 'If you were right, it must have been something that took place a long time ago. You haven't been right since you barged in here. You'd better be careful. I'm practically engaged, you know.'

'Ha!' he commented. 'I see no sign of it.'

He was paying her comments absolutely no attention. Which is what they deserved, she told herself wryly. Why is it that I come up with the best repartee in the world, twenty-four hours after its proper time?

'I shouldn't have said that,' he mused, still staring at her.

'I know you shouldn't have,' she snapped. 'Said what?'

'Said that I wasn't going to do it. Because I am.'

'You am?' she squeaked. His hands locked on to her shoulders again, drawing her hard up against him. 'Yes, I am,' he muttered. And his lips came down on hers a second time. A spark flew between them, like a static discharge. It was a gentle touch, and then suddenly became harsh, demanding. Demanding what, her fevered mind queried. What does he want? His hands shifted from her shoulders, still maintaining the pressure on her lips. One of them wandered down to her waist, forcing her close up against him. The other seemed to hesitate in the middle of her back, and then slid down over her rounded hip.

There's something wrong, her mind hammered at her. In her daze, she barely recognised the message. And then it burst through. He's got his hand——

She struggled against him, beating at his chest with her tiny trapped hands. 'Don't' she gasped weakly. 'Don't do that!'

'Don't do what?' She could see devil-lights in his eyes, sparking at her.

'Don't do *that*,' she snapped at him, using her freed hand to remove his. 'I—that's not a nice thing to do. I don't——'

'Oh come on now,' he grated. 'You've got an eight-year-old child around the house somewhere who demonstrates that you *do*!'

'Why you—you monster!' He had finally ignited her temper. Her right hand swung up in a roundhouse blow, and bounced off his dimple with a very satisfactory crack. It drove him back a step or two—not because of its power, because he was laughing as he moved.

'Okay,' he laughed. 'One for you. I apologise. I didn't mean to say that. I'm sure you don't. And now that I think of it, there was nothing in your news story to cause me to take umbrage.'

'To what?'

'To get mad at you about.'

'Oh.' A silence fell between them. 'You weren't really very nice. I could retract that part of the story.'

'No, I wasn't, was I? I don't know what came over me. How about if I apologise for everything?'

'Everything? About Vicky too?'

'Of course. What's her real name?'

'Victoria. Her father liked that name. I don't know why. There's never been a Victoria in our family before. Just Mary, Kate, Elizabeth—like that.'

'And now Samantha?'

'Oh, that was my dad's choice. He said I was so tiny at my christening that I needed a distinctive name.'

'Your dad? I need to talk to him. When can I meet him?'

'Any time you want. But you have to go to Lebanon to find him. He's a war correspondent. John Clark? Why would you want to see him?'

'That's men's business, girl. You mean this farm houses three women all alone?'

'Oh no—well, not exactly. Grandpa is the head of the house. He's down in New York at a reunion of his World War Two buddies. He'll be back soon. Why?'

'Now that's for me to know, Sam, and you to guess.'

'You talk pretty wild for a strange man, standing in the middle of my bedroom and interrupting all my work. You dog's out back. And that's another thing I want to talk to you about!'

She stomped out of the room ahead of him and clattered down the stairs, her leather sandals slapping at the risers in time with her anger. He hesitated at the top of the stairs and watched. Her long hair bounced from side to side as she walked, her hips swinging in the same rhythm, her straight small back held rigidly, with shoulders squared. 'All good things come in small packages,' he muttered to no-one in particular as he hurried to catch up.

Samantha went directly to her mother's chair. There was a mixed look on the older woman's face. Some concern, some anticipation, some—what? Sam bent over and kissed the smooth cheek.

'I'm alright, Mom,' she whispered. 'He's a strange man. It was the newspaper story that upset him. He read it in the paper this morning. Wait'll you see what they printed! I was never so shocked in my life. They even gave me a by-line. Me! No wonder Mr Bainboro called me. And he said—oops. He said I should try to get another story out of the young man! And I just slapped his face!'

'And he deserved every bit of it!' The voice came over her shoulder, baritone-deep, with a trace of laughter buried within. 'Mrs Clark? We never did get introduced, did we?'

Listen to that, Samantha thought. He's turning on all the charm for my mother. Me, I get the back of his hand. For my mother he pulls out all the stops. And Mother's playing him on!

'It doesn't matter, Mr Clarke? That is it? A bridge man, I understand.'

'Yes,' he laughed, 'but better educated today than I was yesterday. You have a charming daughter. Very good at taking the wind out of pompous sails.'

'Yes.'

'And she has a charming daughter.'

'You mean Vicky? Oh yes indeed. And are you really the man who is going to fix the bridge?'

'You bet. I mean, well, partly. Or else.'

'Why don't you come into the living room and sit down, Mr Clarke?'

'A wonderful idea. But you must call me Jim, ma'am.'

What are you *doing*, Mother, Samantha muttered under her breath. What are you *doing* to me? The two of them had gone in, and arranged themselves opposite each other, ignoring Samantha completely.

'Or else, Mr—Jim?'

'Or else the State may well decide to dispense with my services.'

'You don't look particularly worried about that?' And then, in an aside, 'Sam! Bring Jim a cup of coffee. The poor man must be parched. And so far away from home. Where *is* your home, Jim?'

'In Needham, Mrs Clark. A suburb of Boston, you know. Of course, that's just my apartment. Our family home is on Cape Cod. Are you familiar with . . .'

Their voices faded as Samantha slammed the kitchen door behind her and went over to start the coffee. It helped to slam things a little. DAMN MAN! Making up to my mother like that. Bring him a cup of coffee, Samantha. There's a good girl, Samantha. While he sits in there and makes a play for my *mother*, for heaven's sake. Where did I leave that sprig of mistletoe? If you boil it in plain water, it makes a wonderful poison! Maybe I could slip it into his coffee. DAMN MAN! DAMN DOG! That's it. The dog! Let him struggle with his master for a while!

She flew to the kitchen door. His dog was in exactly the same place where she had left it, three hours before. Collapsed in the sun on one of the warm flaglets of the patio. She stalked over to the slumbering beast.

'Come on Rover,' she urged. The dog lifted its huge head, seemed to blow the hair away from one eye, and examined its tormentor. 'Come on Rover, Rex. Whatever your name is!' The dog had already decided that the conversation was not worth listening to, and lowered its head. 'Come on you!' She threatened, but the dog ignored her.

I don't have to put up with that from both him *and* his dog, Sam raged to herself. She leaned over, got a good grip on the dog's collar, and pulled upward. No results. 'Come on you DAMN DOG,' she roared at it. Both the animal's eyes opened, as if she had struck on the magic word, the open sesame.

'Surely not!' Samantha mumbled. And then, tentatively, 'DAMN DOG?' The huge tail unfolded and began to beat a rhythm on the bricks of the patio. 'Come on, DAMN DOG?' The animal carefully cantilevered itself up on to four feet, waved an agreeable tail, and followed her meekly into the house.

The coffee pot had brewed, and its stand-by light gleamed red in the dark of the kitchen. In the dark? She turned around and looked out. Sure enough, the sun had disappeared, and thunder clouds were billowing up from the west. More trouble. It's Thursday. Vicky will stay after school for music practise, and she'll miss the bus, and it will be raining—and—oh Lord, I'll have to go and get her. Well, first things first.

She set two cups and saucers on the tray. The Noritaki Bone China, she had decided. Putting on the dog. Let him know that we're a cosmopolitan family. World travellers, and all that. Which we really were, until mother was injured. She added the coffee pot to the heavy plastic tray, then changed her mind.

The silver tray was on the top shelf. She pulled a chair over, and used it as a stepping stool. From chair to counter, and then a long stretch. A tiptoe stretch, that just would barely make it. She sighed at her success, until her foot started to slip. She knew what it was before it happened. Vicky had dropped a pat of butter on the counter this morning. I was going to clean it up, her mind yelled at her. I had good intentions! But by that time her foot was well into the butter, her balance was lost, and she fell over backwards with a startled scream. Only to have her downward flight disrupted again by a pair of masculine cable-strong arms.

'We've got to stop meeting like this. People are talking.' He had a big smile on his face. He thinks I'm ridiculous, she stormed at herself. But it felt so—comfortable, that was the word. So comfortable. But the squeezing was not required. She told him so, in no uncertain words.

'Ah, but you're wrong,' he said solemnly. 'There might be bones broken. Like here, for example. Or there!'

'There aren't any bones in either of those places,' she railed at him. 'Put me down, you—lecher!'

'First rule of journalism,' he quipped. 'Never use a word if you can't spell it!'

'Put me down before I scream. And get your hand off my—put me down!'

'Yes, there's always that, isn't there.' He was trying to look mournful, and not succeeding. 'Unless I were to kiss you?'

'No! Don't do that!'

'You won't scream?'

'I—no.'

'Promise?'

'If you promise not to kiss me.' Why am I whispering, she asked herself. What is this hypnotic trick he's using on me?'

'Well, you'd better scream then,' he chuckled. 'I just can't hold off.'

It was another five minutes before they appeared in the living room, he carrying the coffee on a silver tray, she following behind, looking like a girl who had just been thoroughly kissed. Which her mother noted, and did not seem particularly upset about. 'I'm getting to be a kissing expert,' Sam muttered under her breath as she followed him in. And on a scale of one to ten, that one rates about fifteen or so. Poor Charlie. His kisses just couldn't stand up against the competition. But Charlie is my darling, she reminded herself sternly. 'Come on dog!'

What with one thing and another, it hardly surprised Samantha to find that he was invited for lunch, and that her mother intended to carry on a witty conversation with him while her daughter prepared the food. Sam went about it in a haze of emotion, banging pots and pans more than necessary, relieving her frustrations on the dog, who seemed to want to follow her about the house. When she slapped the plates and cutlery on the small table in the dining room, they both looked up, smiling.

'Ready so soon, love?'

'Yes, Mother. Please come.'

'What are we having?' he inquired.

She fought down the rebellious urge to yell 'Peanut butter and jelly sandwiches,' because it wasn't that at all. Her kitchen pride was too great to offer anything but the best. In this case, home-made clam chowder, bread fresh from the oven, and a tossed salad from her own garden vegetables.

Once they were settled down at the table, the private conference between him and her mother continued. Sam sat on the edge of her chair, following along on the edges of the conversation, without much luck. Halfway through, desperate for some attention, she muttered, 'Your dog needs to have her hair clipped. She's a mess.'

He pounced on her immediately. 'Of course she does. Anyone could see that. Why didn't you get it done yesterday?'

'I'm not a hair-dresser for your dog,' she snapped back to him. 'You've really got a nerve, Mr Clarke. You really have!' And since she couldn't think of anything else to say, she slammed her spoon down on the table and stalked out into the kitchen. The dog followed, so close that its nose was brushing her heel as she hurried. She barely made it behind the closed kitchen door when the storm broke, inside and out.

Outside, it was one of those grand performances, a late New England thunder storm. Black clouds billowed thousands of feet high. The wind snatched at everything that grew or moved. Lightning flashed, especially around the stand of pine trees on the hill behind the house, and the thunder rolled long and ominously. And then the rain came. Heavy driving sheets of it, slanting in at the house on its west side, thundering off the kitchens windows, smashing at the little row of climbing roses she had planted next to the patio.

And inside, another storm. She slumped down at the kitchen table and cradled her head in her arms—and cried, without knowing why. The tears flowed as if competing with the rain outside. 'And what am I crying for,' she mumbled to herself. 'He's mean, inconsiderate, impolite, arrogant, loud mouthed, a wheeler-dealer, and I ought to hit him. I ought to hit him again! DAMN MAN!'

The huge dog scrabbled up close to her chair, rested both paws on the table, and began to lick at her tears with a raspy tongue. Sam sniffed, lifted her head to look at her comforter, and smiled through the tears. *'Damn Dog,'* she said tenderly. The huge tail beat on the floor, almost enough to break through the timbers.

They had lunched at one. Her anger had driven her into the kitchen at two. It was almost three before she managed to re-establish her equilibrium, splash liberal amounts of cold water on her face to hide the swollen eyes, and come back into the living room. There he was, all alone, sitting in her father's chair, with his feet up on the ottoman, reading her grandfather's favourite magazine. He put it down when he heard her come in.

'Your mother had to go for her nap,' he said solemnly. 'We thought you had gone out into the back yard to eat worms.' Which was the old New England expression used about people who go off into corners to sulk.

'Thank you,' she said, with only the faintest amount of enthusiasm. 'Don't let me keep you from anything you planned for the day. Don't you have to work? Neither snow, nor rain, and so forth?'

'That's for postmen,' he returned. 'Civil Engineers don't work in the rain. Union rules.'

'Huh!'

'Is that the best you can do?'

'Yes it is,' she snarled at him. 'I'm not as brilliant a conversationalist as my mother.'

'Perhaps not.' He smiled. He actually smiled at her. 'But you've got a prettier figure. And when you walk, lady—oh have you got it!' One of his hands came up behind her and tapped her gently on her well-rounded bottom.

'What is it with you,' she snapped, backing off to a safer distance. 'Do you have a fetish, or something?

Every time you get near me you have to get you hand on my—on me. Stop it!'

'Yes, of course,' he said mournfully. 'A terrible hangover from my deprived youth. I shall certainly try to curb my excesses. Does that suit you, lady?'

'Nothing suits me about you. Are you leaving?'

'I hadn't planned to. Your mother invited me to stay.'

She glared at him suspiciously. 'Are you making a play for my *mother*? She's married, you know. And my dad is a big mean man. He'd make two of you!'

'See me tremble,' he said in that same mournfully tone. 'It's always that way. It seems to be my fate to be misunderstood.'

'No wonder. You need a new script-writer. Your dialogue sounds as if it came out of a nineteen-sixteen melodrama.'

'See what I mean,' he continued. 'Always misunderstood. My real purpose, Samantha Clark, is to get you to take me in hand and reform me—and my dog, of course.'

'Take you?' She could feel her voice rise in hysterical response. 'I wouldn't take you for *anything*. I could certainly do better with your damn dog!'

'Ah. You *did* learn her name. Wonderful. Where are you going?'

'I'm going out and get in my car, and go down to the Regional school to pick up Vicky.'

'Your daughter Victoria?'

'My daughter Vicky. Why don't you take advantage of my absence and disappear? I would consider it a great favour. And it's the only one I intend to ask of you!'

To make sure she had the last word, she slammed out of the living room, snatched her poncho from the coatrack by the front door, and went out in the driving rain to her car. Where she sat and ground the starter, and watched nothing happen. And ground the starter again and again, until eventually even the starter-motor refused to budge. 'Lousy battery!' She yelled as she beat on the steering wheel with her tiny hands. By that time her digital wrist watch indicated 2:55, and she knew she had either to commit Hara Kiri, or ask for his help.

'You're asking me for a favour?' he prodded as he helped her into his fancy little car. 'I thought you were never going to ask me for a favour again?'

'Alright, so I was wrong,' she muttered. 'I—I tend to get excited, and perhaps sometimes I say things that I ought not to— and ...' She turned her head very determinedly to her right, and glared out the side window at the scenery she had loved all her life.

'And I take it that's all the apology I'm going to get?'

Laugh at me. Go ahead and laugh at me, she screamed to herself. One little titter—one little noise, and so help me, I'll beat up on you to the death! But then gradually, her commonsense returned. Sure I will, she told herself. Look at us! She sidled a little closer to the outer edge of the bucket seat. Look at us! The top of my head comes under his shoulder. If he were to fall over on top of me, it would squash me half to death. What a way to go! And the giggles that broke out startled them both. And I don't even know if I like him, she thought, but ...

CHAPTER THREE

HE brought them back to the farm with a flourish that tickled Vicky's heart. The little girl had been talking to him ten miles to the minute during the whole trip, while Samantha, sharing the bucket seat, had done her best to keep out of things. She watched him out of the corner of her eyes. He's looking at me as if he were a hired mourner at the funeral, she thought. What is it about that look? Those deep blue eyes? The crinkle just by his nose. At least now I can see he's not *perfect*, and that's a relief. And then Vicky's chatter intruded on her thoughts.

'It's something I've been thinking about all day,' the girl was saying. 'It sure would be easy for you, Mom.'

And like a fool, she was unable to leave it alone. 'Easy what?' she asked. And then recognised her foolishness, and bit down on her lower lip so that no more words could escape. How can I be a reporter when I'm so stupid with words, she demanded of herself. I wish I could talk as well as I can write!

By now they had stepped out of the rain into the hall, and were busy shucking their rainwear. 'Well,' Vicky continued, 'all you would have to do is add an *e* on your name, and you and him could be all married. That would be kind of nice.'

'How true,' he echoed. 'How very true.'

She looked up at him, startled. Is it possible that he really could mean something like that? That glint was still lurking in his eyes. Of course not, she told herself angrily. Impossible. All he really wants is—what the devil *does* he want? I know, but I don't want to admit it! Her face turned blush-red. Both her fists clenched. She squeezed them tightly against her breasts. Nothing would make her mother more angry than to find out that she had hit him again! 'Who put those silly ideas in your head,' she snapped at Vicky.

'Nobody put nothin' nowhere,' the child protested. 'I thunk it up all by myself. Why—why you're really mad, Sam! Why are you mad?'

She tried to explain, but failed. Nothing came out but gibberish. She was actually choking on words! What in the world does he do to me to make me feel like this? I—I've *got* to get out of here!

With new determination she shoved her way by him and made for the kitchen, slamming the door behind her. I'm not going to cry, she told herself sternly. I'm not going to cry. He can't make me cry! I won't let it happen.

From out in the hall, filtered through her confused mind, she could hear the soft tones of her mother's soothing voice, the high-pitch of happiness in Vicky's, the deep counter-point of his. The words were too faint to be decoded. But I know one thing, she told herself. *They're* all happy. So why am *I* hiding in the kitchen, doing my best not to cry?

And then a new thought gave her conscience a quick kick. Get a new story from him, Mr Bainsboro had said. Not a suggestion. Not a request. An order. Get a new story from him. Back to the cold water tap she went. Lots of cold water, especially around the eyes. Then pat-dry the whole affair. Check your hair, you idiot. And hurry. He may leave any minute now! But I—I can't go out looking like this. I have to—and even as she argued with herself her busy fingers were plaiting her soft hair into a single braid, which she left to hang down in front, over her left shoulder. Repairs completed, she made for the kitchen door, hesitating just long enough to congratulate herself. He *hadn't* made her cry, had he? She brushed down her blouse, affixed a smile, and went through to the living room.

'Better, Mom?' Vicky was sitting crosslegged in front of her grandmother's wheelchair.

'Yes, love, I'm better. I got a frog caught in my throat, is all.'

'You overdo,' her mother cautioned her as she reached out a welcome hand. Samantha walked over to the chair, bent, and kissed the proffered cheek. 'It was good of Mr Clarke—er—Jim—to run you down to the school'

'Mama didn't think it was so good,' Vicky added. 'She got mad and cried. I guess I never will understand grown-ups if I live to be a hundred.'

'No, of course not,' he agreed. 'Understanding grown-ups is a terrible problem. And now that I see Sam doesn't intend murder or suicide, I think I'd better run along. It's not true what I said, Sam. Engineers *do* have to work in the rain at times!'

'I told you about that,' the child interrupted again. 'Don't call her Sam. She don't like no men to call her Sam? I try so hard to get you trained right, and then you spoil it! Don't you never call her Sam!'

'Ah! I've messed up again, have I?' He was talking to the child, but staring at Samantha. 'Well, is it such a terrible crime?'

'No,' Sam sputtered. 'No, of course not. I—you——' She forced herself to break contact with his eyes, pinning her downturned vision on her twisting hands. 'No, Mr Clarke, and besides, I wanted to ask a favour of you?'

'Done,' he laughed. 'What else?'

'You haven't heard what it is yet,' she snapped. 'Maybe you won't like it!'

'If it's for Samantha Clark, it's done,' he repeated. And then, as if it were an afterthought, 'Or is it for that reporter?'

'It's for the reporter,' she sighed. 'My editor wants me to do another story about the bridge, and about—er . . .'

'And about that nice young engineer?'

'I—I'm afraid so. About that nice young engineer and his bridge. Please?'

He hesitated. His eyes roamed around the room and then came back to her. 'Right,' he said. 'Even for that damn reporter. Just so long as you remember, I'm doing it as a favour for the Clark family.'

'Of course,' she muttered. You mean for my mother,

don't you. You've got a thing going for my mother, and you're using Vicky and me as a way to get at her! I *know* she's still beautiful, and only forty-five years old. With lots more poise and character than me. And better educated, and more sophisticated. Oh God, why do I torture myself like this! Alright, wise-guy, I'll fix your little red wagon for you! Wait until you read my *next* story.

'Tomorrow,' he told her, as she helped him on with his lightweight coat. 'I'll pick you up about ten in the morning, and we'll go and look at the bridge together.'

'Alright,' she agreed. 'Ten o'clock. I'll be ready.' She held the outer door open for him. 'The rain has stopped,' she commented, and immediately felt like a fool. He can see! You don't have to tell him about the weather! And then, as he started down the stairs. 'Oh! You forgot your dog!'

He turned and glared at her. 'I didn't forget,' he growled. 'She won't come. She's upstairs in your bedroom, sleeping on your rug. I think she's decided she likes life better with you than with me. Get her hair trimmed!'

'Why—you ...! You ungratefully arrogant, odious man!' But he was already climbing into his car as she spoke, and must have missed it all. 'And just when I had a good line,' she muttered to herself. He waved at her as the car began to move. She stepped back and slammed the front door as hard as she could. 'So there!' she yelled at the unlistening world.

'And what was that all about?' her Mother inquired from the living room door.

'That man!' Samantha snorted. 'That horrible rotten—civil servant!'

'You mean Mr Clarke?'

'Yes, I mean Mr Clarke. I have never in my life seen such an arrogant—why are you laughing at me, Mother?'

'Because, my dear, that's exactly the way your father appeared to me on our first date. No one in the world was more astonished than I to find myself marrying him. Come into the living room and calm down, love. I want to talk about something.'

'Well, you can't tell me that that horrible man is anything like my father!' She stomped into the living room and plopped herself down on the sofa, hugging one of the pillows to her stomach. Count to one hundred, she told herself. Your mother has gone bananas over that—that man. Calm down. One, two, three——

'I want to talk about Vicky.' Her mother's soft voice penetrated the void on second repetition.

'About Vicky?' It was the last subject in the world she had expected to hear.

'Yes dear. It's about this *mother* thing she's got going with you. Don't you think it's about time to correct that? Oh, I know it had a good purpose in the beginning, and you were wonderful to shoulder the burden. But she's settled down now. You are *not* her mother, and if you allow it to go on much longer, you may very well find it an intolerable burden. Especially if you meet some nice young man. Men are not that tolerant about accepting somebody else's child you know.'

'The man who marries me will accept Vicky,' Sam said in a quiet determined tone. 'It'll be all or nothing. And I'll make that plain to him before we get too far down the pike.' She stopped to muse for a moment, and then continued slowly. 'We talked about it right after her birthday party. And she still needs me. As her mother, I mean. No, as long as she has that need, I shall never stop being her mother. I don't know how long that will be—but as long as it takes. I won't change things. Besides, it's not all one-sided, love. It was all her idea in the beginning, but now it's a two-way street. She wants me to mother her—and I get a good feeling out of doing it. We both profit. Just today she mentioned that she remembered Kate. And that's what it's for, isn't it? For Vicky, for me, and for Kate? She was the finest sister any girl could have. You know that. She was the assistant mother around this place for years. Especially when you were able to go overseas with Dad. So it's a sort of full-circle fulfillment. Kate was my stand-in mother, and I am determined to be Vicky's. For however long she needs me.'

'But Sam! One of these days, when we get things cleared up, and I get on my feet again, you'll want to go off to a university, just the way you planned. And then what about Vicky?'

'I don't think so, Mom. These last years have changed my goals in life. I don't think about university any more.'

'Oh Sam!' Her mother's sigh was almost enough to make her change her mind. 'Your father and I had such great plans for you, and now you're all we have. Is it definitely to be Charlie Aikens? What if you were to fall in love with—oh, Jim Clarke, for example?'

'I'm not sure about Charlie, but Jim Clarke is preposterous, Mother. I'd sooner run off with the milkman than marry Clarke. What the devil would I want to do that for? A down-at-the heels engineer? He could lose his job tomorrow, you know. Civil Service isn't what it is cracked up to be. Not any more!'

When Sam looked up, there was no doubt about it! Now her *mother* was laughing at her! 'What in the world?' she asked.

'It's you, love,' her mother chuckled, wiping her eyes. 'I never thought I would be raising my daughter to be a snob. Besides, Mr Clarke isn't a Civil Servant. He's an outside consultant, hired by the State to examine several bridges and make recommendations. He and his father own a very expensive engineering firm up in Boston.'

'Sure he does,' Sam returned sarcastically. 'Is that what he told you? Oh, what a glib one he is. You mustn't be taken in by what he says, Mother. He's very slick. You don't have enough experience with men to play in this man's league. Be careful!'

'Me?' Her mother was laughing wholeheartedly now. 'You think—oh Samantha—you think he's chasing me?'

'No, of course not,' she answered stonily. 'Why else would he spend the entire day chatting you up, I ask. You're still a fine figure of a woman, Mother.'

'Well of course I'll be careful,' her mother returned, in that soft persuasive voice that one uses with young children and mental defectives. 'I'll be very careful, Sam. And you must be, too, of course.'

'Me? Why me?'

'I admit I don't have as much experience with young men as you do, Samantha, but somehow in the back of my mind is the thought that he might be hunting someone exactly like you. Just be careful, that all. Oops, I forgot to put the potatoes on.'

Sam was about to say something terribly important, but lost track of it in the shuffle that followed. But as her hands worked over the supper, her mind still squirreled. Charlie Aikens? We've been sweethearts all our lives—but, marriage? Now that Clarke fellow, what in the devil does *he* want? I don't seem to understand anybody anymore. It isn't bad enough that I have to worry about Clarke, now I have to put my mother on the worry list too. But isn't it rather plain what *he* wants? Every time he comes near he puts his hands on me, and then his eyes light up like a pinball machine spinning out a triple-win. What *he* wants is to persuade stupid little Samantha into his bed! And *that* stupid I am not! Now who the devil could be ringing the doorbell at this time of day? Damn! Damn! Damn!

She squirmed out of her apron and started slowly for the door. The bell rang twice more. She put on a burst of speed and opened it before it rang again. 'Charlie!' Her mind was so confused that she welcomed the normality of his narrow freckled face, and threw her arms around his neck. Sam was not usually so emotional, but even on the spur of the moment, he managed a comfortable kiss.

'Well that's some welcome, Samantha.' He looked like a man who had forgotten a birthday or anniversary—and didn't dare ask which it was. She stepped back and smiled gently at him. Charlie Aikens.

Five-foot-eight in the vertical, and hardly enough of
him to measure in the horizontal. Two years older than
she. A hard working friend and neighbour, who would
one day inherit a fine farm. But do you love him? Her
mind didn't want to know the answer. Not now. 'Oh,
your typing,' she said.

'Charlie, I feel terrible about it, but I haven't finished
your work yet. This is terrible.'

'Not really, Samantha. I do need it, but I don't mind
waiting around for a while.'

'I don't mean quite that,' she hastened to assure him.
'I mean there's a great deal of it left to be done. I'll tell
you what I'll do, Charlie. Right after supper I'll get at it
and finish it up. And I'll bring it over to your
house——' She was about to say 'tonight,' but had
second thoughts. Aikens lived all alone in a separate
cottage on his father's farm. There were no neighbours
within a mile or more. And with all this encouragement, her arrival in the middle of the night would be
just the most stupid thing she could do.

'Tomorrow morning,' she compromised. 'Early.
While I'm taking Vicky to school.' Which ought to
make it about as safe as one could get, she told herself.

'Well, okay,' he said slowly. 'Oh, your flag was up so
I emptied the mailbox for you.' With the ponderous
deliberation that was his usual speed he handed her a
miscellaneous bunch of envelopes. She tendered effusive
thanks, received a kiss on the cheek due to fast
manoeuvre, and ushered him out the door.

'Who was that, Sam?' Vicky clattered down the
stairs from her usual relaxation, watching television.
Grandfather Clark hated the electronic showmen, so
there was no television downstairs. One bedroom on
the floor above had been converted into a play and
work room for rainy days. It held Vicky's TV set, the
family sewing machine, and Grandfather's stamp
collection.

'Oh, just Charlie Aikens,' she replied, as she sorted
through the mail. 'He wanted to pick up his
paperwork.'

'Hah!' the little girl returned. 'He wanted to pick *you* up. Any mail for me?'

'Not you too,' Sam groaned. Are they all watching me like that? Even the child knows more than I do about the men around me. Out of the mouths of babes?

'Hey, are you in luck today, baby. You have a letter from your grandfather in Lebanon!'

Vicky squealed with delight. 'Gimme,' she yelled. 'Grandma! Grandma! I got a letter from Grandpa!' She bounced up on to the couch, folding her legs under her, and prepared to hold court. Samantha lay the other unexamined envelopes down on the coffee table and coiled herself up on the floor. Moments later her mother whisked herself in from her room. 'From your Grandpa? Go ahead—read it!'

Supper that night was filled with discussion, cut short when Samantha realized how many hours lay ahead of her before she could finish up Aikens's typing work. It was midnight before the last form was slipped into the last envelope, and the whole piled into a manilla folder, ready for delivery in the morning. She got up from her chair and stretched lazily, trying to get the crick out of her neck, and then opted for a long hot bath to complete the job. All in all, she chuckled, as she slid her satin froth of a nightgown over her head, it has been a strange day.

Sleep was hard to come by. Dream followed dream, until her sheets were so twisted that she finally climbed out of bed to straighten things out. A cool September moon hung low over the farmhouse, glazing everything in silver. The storm had cleared the sky and sprinkled it with stars. It seemed a good omen. She went down to the kitchen, with the dog padding behind her, and shared warm milk. Then back to bed. The dog felt her restlessness, and moved to lay her head on the blankets. Samantha ruffled the animal's neck, scratched behind one big ear, and finally fell asleep.

Morning came too soon and not much welcomed. At least, not by Sam. Only duty drove her out of bed. Duty and Vicky, dancing wildly around her bed and chanting some stupidity about Chief Crazy Horse, come to sacrifice a maiden.

'Where in the world do you get that kind of talk,' she grumbled as she swung her legs out on to the floor.

'From the TV. Where else?' The little girl executed a couple more experimental whoops and then, when threatened, dashed for the door.

Samantha managed to make breakfast with only one eye open, fed the chickens, and stumbled back to the kitchen. At seven her mother rolled down the hall, smiling like a Cheshire cat.

'You had a good night, Mother?' *Lord how I hate to talk to cheery people when I'm so grouchy,* she thought.

'Very nice,' her mother murmured. 'What do you think? I went to sleep with your father's letter under my pillow, and I dreamed that he was coming home soon, and that I—oh well, that part is private. What's the hurry?'

'I have to drive Vicky to school today. And there's some material I have to drop off at Charlie's house. And then that—Mr Clarke is coming by for me at ten o'clock. We're going to tour the bridge. You knew the paper asked for another story?'

'That was a pretty naughty story you did the last time, Sam. You must always be impersonal with your stories. That's what your father always said. French Toast? Oh how wonderful. It's been ages since we had French Toast.'

'Yes,' Samantha agreed, turning back to the skillet. 'I just can't remember why we stopped having it.'

She soon recalled. Vicky clattered down the stairs, all polished and dressed, pulled out a chair next to her grandmother, and looked down at the plate. 'French Toast?' she groaned. 'Uggh!'

'Oh, by the way,' her mother commented in passing, 'one of those letters yesterday was for you, Sam.' There was too much to be done at the moment, so she crammed the letter into the pocket of her dress.

So all in all it was a rather short-tempered Samantha who sat on the porch glider at ten o'clock, waiting for her Engineer to drive up. He came promptly on the hour. She walked down to the car immediately, not wanting to let him at her mother again. As she climbed into the bucket seat of his car he favoured her with one of those big wide grins. 'How's my dog?'

She stopped to look around. 'Why, she was just here with me a second or two ago,' she said, puzzled. 'She must have got up and walked off just——'

'Yeah, I know,' he chuckled. 'Just as soon as she heard me coming. That dog has a terrible crush on you, Samantha Clark. I may have to sue you for alienation of affection.' And then he subjected her to another one of those radar-scans of his. 'Hey, you don't plan to go bridge-watching in that get-up, do you?'

'Well!' There wasn't another word she could think of. She had gone to great lengths to look feminine today. Her dirndle skirt, of cranberry-patterned cotton, swung satisfactorily around her legs. Her square-draped blouse with the lace inserts was cut low enough to display somewhat more than the tops of her firm breasts, and her hair was done up in double braids, pinned up in a coronet around her head. To top it all off, her favourite fluffy cardigan was slung over her shoulders, held by a single button. Everything considered, she thought she looked rather well!

'So wear what you want,' he said, breaking the dangerous silence that had fallen between them. The little car squealed as he hit the accelerator. They did a screeching U-turn, and hurried down Mattapoisett Road in the general direction of Route Six.

He merged into the traffic and headed west. The tide was low as they approached the bridge. The strong smell of sea weed pinched at her nostrils as the wind picked up slightly. The brilliant sun, playing tag with a few white cumulous clouds, added a sparkle. Gradually her day began to improve.

He stopped at Marine Park again, on the island that formed the central section of the crossing. Before she left the shelter of the car Samantha wound her paisley scarf around her head. He was smiling as he offered a hand to help her out. She didn't plan to accept, but had to anyway. Short people and bucket seats just don't go together, she mused. The wind played at her skirts but she managed her exit from the car without too much display. He seemed rather disappointed. So did the seagull that dived at them, and then sheared away.

'You could let go of my hand,' she suggested, when she managed to get both feet on the ground. He didn't seem to hear. He was looking north up the bay. 'Up there,' he pointed with his free hand to the place about a mile up-river, where narrows constricted the flood. 'Now that's the place for a bridge. A new one, right where that causeway is located. All the boat traffic would be south of it, and we could build a simple fixed span. With a good bridge up there it would be silly to try to do something with this old clinker.'

'Silly?' she snapped. 'And what about all the Fairhaven merchants?'

'Come off it,' he chuckled. 'This is a mobile world we live in. A total detour of three or four miles wouldn't mean a hill of beans to shoppers. And think how much traffic it would keep off the streets of the town. That would be a godsend.'

'And what about the merchants along the bridge itself? They've been here for as long as the bridge has!'

'And we should spend many many millions to rebuild a bridge in the wrong place, just so a few people can stay in business? That's the way a politician designs a bridge, not an engineer. The only reason for building the new bridge on this site is because you've always had a bridge here. And that's one stupid argument, lady. A fixed bridge up north there would cost one quarter as much, and require fifty per cent less maintenance. Hey, come out here and look.'

He dragged her out to the edge of the sidewalk, almost thrusting her into the busy street. 'Look straight over there and up.' He was pointing her towards the hillside up which the City of New Bedford sprawled. 'Now, see that—that apartment building just off to the right?'

'The Melville Towers? That's public housing for the elderly. It's only been there for—oh—ten years at the most. So?'

'So if we put in this high-rise bridge the Commissioner was talking about, all that would have to go. We would have to start the approaches about half-way up that hill. And that would mean either demolish that row of multi-storey houses over on that side, or knock off that yellow-brick thing in front of them, along with that bronze brick building behind it. How about that?'

'Why——' The concept was too much for her to grasp. 'That's the new Federal Building, and the new courthouse. They just finished that this year. That's impossible. You can't do that!'

'Me? I can't do that? I'm only the consultant, lady. All the State is asking from me is advice.'

'And what are you going to advise them?'

'Well, I don't know, do I? But the first step has to be to patch up this old wreck. Let's go have a look.'

He started at a determined hundred miles an hour, still holding her hand. 'For goodness sakes,' she gasped, 'slow down! My legs aren't anywhere near as long as yours.'

'Spoilsport,' he laughed. 'I thought all you New England witches could fly.' But he did slow his pace to match her own. She started to make small talk, but the buzz of passing cars, the sweep of the breeze, and the screaming of the gulls, all were against it. Besides, as they walked, his eyes were continually searching from side to side, and she could almost see his mind piling up mental notes as they went along.

The sound from under their feet changed as they left the concrete of the fixed section of the bridge, and moved on to the steel tresselway. Things acquired an echo, and looking down through the patterned metal, she could see the water of the harbour surging around the mass of concrete and steel that supported the centre of the bridge.

He led her to the exact centre, then helped her to the railing. 'Take a good look,' he said. 'Boats have the right-of-way. When a boat whistles, the bridge is swung sideways, balancing on this central foundation. It opens a channel of about ninety feet on each side. Ninety feet of usable space for the boats, that is. But this central core takes up sixty feet all by itself. It's a terrible waste of a good channel.'

'That's a tremendous weight,' she suggested hesitantly. 'How do they move it?'

'Hydraulic pumps,' he returned. 'The centre of the bridge is mounted on some very large bearings, and water pressure is used to move it, and to partially support it. In the nineteen-thirties it was modernised, and we now have a hermaphrodite rig. The hydraulic pumps do all the work, but they themselves are powered electrically.'

'But—if the bridge is open, how do you get electricity out here?'

He gave her one of those 'where have you been for the past fifty years' looks. 'A cable,' he told her. 'An underwater cable. It comes out from the New Bedford side, goes underwater in the channel, and comes up on the base, right about there.' He gestured down below them, at something she could not quite see.

'Well, come on,' he said quietly, taking her arm just below the elbow.

'Come on where?'

'We came to inspect the bridge, so let's inspect it.'

'Down there?' she gasped, looking at the narrow ladder that led through the interstices of the bridge down towards the water, some twenty feet below them.

'No, not down there,' he laughed. 'Up there.' Her head snapped back. Above her stretched a wildly symmetrical lacing of cables and metal struts that towered a good forty feet high, and stretched from one end of the moveable section to the other.

'I—I don't want to go up there!' she managed to sputter. There was just no way that she would tell him she suffered from acrophobia—the fear of heights!

'We have to,' he insisted. 'That's what I have to inspect. What happened to the brave female reporter? Up we go.'

'Up where?'

'Can you see that little hut up there on the top? No, not there, on the very top.'

'That little shack?'

'That little shack. What's the matter? Scared?'

'No!' You might as well sound firm about it, she told herself. You know darn well you're scared half to death. Climb up there? No power on earth could drive me to climb up there! Then why am I walking sedately along with him towards the ladder?

'There's no lift?' she managed.

'Nope. Footpower. Here are the steps. Up you go!'

Here are the steps. Indeed! The whole thing looked like a scrawny open-work fire escape, with narrow risers, a steep ascent, and a pair of rickety metal handrails. There was no pretention towards dignity or safety. I don't want to go up there, she raged to herself. I don't! But her hands moved to the handrails, and she had taken two full steps upward when the wind came rattling at her skirts again. Her face turned brilliant red, and she dropped back off the stairs.

'No you don't, smart aleck,' she told him. 'If we have to go up that thing, you go first.'

'No, we can't do it that way.' He was trying to appear solemn, and not quite making it. That crazy dimple was jumping around, heralding a real laugh. 'You have to go first,' he assured her. 'It's a safety problem. If you should slip, or lose your grip, then I'll be right there to catch you.'

'Yes, I'll bet you would,' she snarled. 'If I climb up that thing in front of you, you'll be so busy looking up under my skirts that you couldn't catch rainwater if I provided the bucket. Not on your life, James Clarke.'

'Say, you've got an exaggerated sense of modesty,' he returned. 'You'd rather risk your neck than show me what colour panties you're wearing?'

'You'd better just believe it!'

'It hardly seems worth the struggle,' he mused. 'Sooner or later I'm going to find out, Samantha Clark. Why not give up gracefully?'

'Sometimes you make me boil over,' she roared at him. 'I—you   '

'Okay, I'm going!' He swung himself up the stairs as if it were an ordinary daily chore. Sam took a deep breath, said a prayer, closed her eyes, and began to toil upward after him. Every few steps he stopped and waited for her. And if he makes on crack about how far it is, she told herself, I'll skewer him for Sunday dinner! Perhaps he could read the threat, for he said nothing.

It took ten minutes for her to complete the climb. Only the urging of his hands had made the last ten feet possible. She was terribly thankful when he clambered down around her, came up from below, and pressed himself against her back while she climbed. All thought of modesty had fled in the face of an engulfing fear. When she tumbled through the door of the little wooden cabin, and it closed behind them, she gave one big sigh of relief and collapsed on the couch that filled up one wall. Another five minutes passed before she caught her breath, and there he was with a glass of something wet in his hand.

'Lemonade,' he said. And then she noted the little refrigerator, the tiny propane stove, the water tank. 'All the amenities, including a chemical toilet,' he gestured. 'In the old days the bridge tender stayed up here all the time, fair weather and foul.'

'And now?'

'Well, sometimes they operate from up here. Most of the time, though, they used that little building on the New Bedford side of the bridge. See it?'

She moved nervously to the window beside him and peered down at the foreshortened world. 'I—I didn't realise how high it would be,' she sniffed. 'I'm not sure I can get down again.'

'Not to worry,' he chuckled. 'If you decide you can't get down, we'll just have to camp out up here. There are enough rations to last a couple of days.'

'Hah!' she snorted. 'Up here with you? Not a chance, Mr Clarke. Well, aren't you going to inspect things?'

'I will. I will. Right after you tell me.'

'Right after I tell you what?'

'Right after you tell me about this man you're engaged to.'

'Why—why you!' she sputtered. 'You brought me all this way——! Alright. His name is Charlie. He's a fine man, about my age, and we've been going around together since I was twelve years old. He isn't—brash or arrogant, or—he's going to own a farm—and he's just—nice!'

'And when is the wedding to be?'

'I—we—haven't set a date yet,' she stammered. Haven't set a date? Charlie hasn't even asked, her conscience prodded. But he will, she assured herself. Just any time I want him to. 'But it will be soon,' she continued, trying to reinforce her courage. 'Very soon!'

'Do you suppose if I owned a farm I would have a chance?' There was that wide grin on his face again. 'Or maybe if I were younger?' The grin was still there, but deep in those eyes there was a gleam of frustration, of bitterness.

'Fat chance,' she snapped. 'Charles and I are deeply committed.'

'Ah, but there's nothing to stop us from having a little affair before the wedding, is there?' His face was all steel now. Stern bitter steel. Step into my parlour said the spider to the fly.

CHAPTER FOUR

SAMANTHA was too shocked to respond. She stood there in the middle of the hut, her face as white as death, her tiny hands clenched so tightly at her sides that her nails were biting into her flesh.

'Alright, alright.' He was trying to sooth her, to calm her down. 'I didn't mean to insult you.' He dropped one arm across her shoulders. She shuddered away from his touch, backing up against the couch, and then sidling away as she recognised what her knees were touching.

'My God,' he muttered. 'A touch-me-not? Are you so wrapped up in this unmarried mother bit that it colours everything you do?'

'And are you so wrapped up in your great macho male image that you can't leave a girl alone? I don't like being mauled by older men!'

'Is that what's disturbing you?' To her absolute surprise he burst out laughing, a full-throated roar of enjoyment that set her scalp tingling. He trapped her in the corner, seized both her shoulders, and seated her unceremoniously on the couch. 'Now just sit there, spitfire,' he roared at her. 'You and I have a lot to talk about.'

'No, we certainly do not,' she snapped back at him. She bounced to her feet and ran to the door. He wasn't following. The door knob turned clumsily in her hands, and it creaked open. She took one look down that open stairway, and knew immediately that she could never climb down alone. Two deep breaths restored her control. Shaking her head dolefully, she turned back to him.

'It's a long way down, isn't it?' he queried, head cocked to one side. 'And you are just a little bit afraid of heights, aren't you? Better come and sit down.'

There seemed to be nothing left to do. Against her will, her feet dragging as she moved, her body took command and guided her back to the couch she had so recently abandoned. She plopped down on to the aging springs, positioned her hands primly in her lap, and wished, for dignity's sake, that her feet could touch the floor.

'Well, how did you know I don't—I . . . How did you know?'

'That you have a fear of high places? What the devil did you think your mother and I have been talking about all this time, Sam?'

'Don't call me Sam. I detest it.'

'I like it. All the time we were talking, Sam, the subject was you. From cute Samantha Clark, the tiniest baby your family had ever seen, all the way through high school. I know everything there is to know about you, Samantha, from your impacted wisdom tooth to your expensive taste in underwear. From your first boyfriend, to your latest newspaper ambitions. Everything. How about that?'

'Everything. You really mean everything? She told you about Vicky?'

'How about that!' He looked surprised. 'That makes two things we overlooked. I never even thought to ask. Come to think of it, she never even mentioned your little indiscretion. For all I heard, you might have found Vicky under a bush. Did you?'

'Yes I did,' she snarled at him. 'She was a foundling.'

'Who just happens to look exactly like you.'

'Yes!' Smart aleck! I wouldn't tell you the real story now if you paid me a steamer-trunk full of hundred dollar bills. See what you can make out of that, damn you!'

'I don't happen to believe you,' he laughed. 'It just doesn't fit your character. But that's not what I want to hear about. I've adjusted to that little quirk already. Tell me about your mother.'

'Her accident, you mean?' He nodded Samantha tried a couple more deep breaths. At their height above the bay it was clean salt air, blowing gently through cracks in the doorframe.

'I—I think we have to—to talk about my sister, first,' she said. 'It's all part of it—of everything.'

'So okay, tell me about your sister. I didn't know you had one.'

'Don't you have to check something, or inspect something?'

'I'm doing that. Stop stalling. Start talking. You're worse than Damn Dog.'

'I have—I had—a sister. She was ten years older than me. Her name was Kate. Katherine. She went—on a trip. In an airplane. And never came back. All that love and devotion, just extinguished. With no warning, no preparation. Just went out the door and never came back!' The memory of it all overwhelmed her. She sat there, with her back rigid, her head held up high, and the tears rolled down her cheeks and splashed off her chin.

'Alright, little soldier, let them come.' He was beside her on the couch, his warm arm around her, pulling her over until her nose was buried in his soft sweater. 'Cry it out,' he whispered in her ear. 'Cry it out, love.' So she did. Momemts later, reduced to mere sniffles, she looked up at him over the borrowed handkerchief. It's getting to be a habit, she lectured herself. Every time I see him I end up crying. I wish I knew what it is. It can't be hate, because I don't hate him. And it can't be love, because love is supposed to make you happy. So what is it?

She dabbed at her eyes, knowing what a sight they must be, and managed to hold her breath long enough to break up the hiccups that always threatened her after a good cry. The flood's over, her conscience told her. You ought to move away from him. Sam! Samantha! But neither person was paying attention. She sat close, warmed and cheered, and almost dry-eyed.

'And that——' she cleared her throat noisily, and started again. 'And that was the first accident. We're a very superstitious family. All bad things happen in three's. And so then Mama slipped in the bath tub. She was trying to stand up, and she slipped and fell on her back. And became paralysed from the waist down.'

'The doctors couldn't do anything about it?'

'They couldn't then. They can now. That's why Dad hurried off to Beirut. He's too old for that sort of thing, but they pay combat bonuses, and we need the money.'

'For what?'

'For the operation, of course. We have no Blue Cross coverage. Dad always liked to work freelance, and its difficult, not being a member of some large organisation, to get medical insurance. We have some, but not enough. We have to scrape up sixty thousand dollars, to cover the rest of the costs, before they'll operate.'

'So that's why you work as a reporter, and type insurance forms.'

'And can fruits to sell, and baby sit. And do anything possible to make another nickel. The longer we wait, the worse her chances are. Dad and Grandpa and I— but you know what I make is like a grain of sand on a beach. I just don't know, and I'm afraid. I'm afraid we may wait too late, or Pops could get himself shot, or Grandpa could get so desperate that he'd sell the farm. Sometimes I just get so tired thinking about it, that——'

She looked up, to find his face so close that it had gone out of focus, but nothing mattered any more. She closed her eyes and cuddled closer, looking for comfort. And found it.

It was a very subdued girl that followed his directions, a half-hour later, as they made their way down the steep stairs. He went first, just a step below her. Close enough so that his comfortable frame pressed against her. 'Don't look down,' he kept telling her. 'Close your eyes if it bothers. Put your hands on my shoulders and lean against me, love.'

It had a nice sound to it. Lean against me, love. All her small fears seemed to have disappeared. She actually opened her eyes and watched as the beauty of the bay deployed itself before her. A seaplane was taking off just to her left, scattering the platoons of gulls who owned the area. Two stern trawlers were tailing each other out into the Sound, *en route* to the fishing grounds on the Grand Banks. A trim Coast Guard cutter was manoeuvring into its berth at the State Pier. She was smiling when finally her foot touched the metal of the bridge's lower platform.

She stepped away from him long enough to smooth down her errant skirt, and to more securely pin her plaits in place. His hand stopped hers, removing the hairgrips she had inserted, and letting her hair fall loose. It flew wild in the wind, back from her head, and then dropped in a swathe around her face when the breeze died.

'I like it that way,' he said firmly.

'I don't!' There was just enough rebellion left in her to resent his dictatorial ways.

'But you'll wear it that way for me.' It wasn't a question, just a quiet order. One that he seemed to know she would follow. And if he wasn't surprised, she was, to hear herself say, 'Yes, of course.' They walked back off the bridge to his car, arm in arm, without exchanging another word.

As he handed her into the car, he said, 'so far that's two accidents in your family. What do you suppose the third will be?'

She ducked her head, swinging her hair around to hide her too-expressive face. He walked around the hood of the car, and surely couldn't hear her as she mumbled, half-statement, half-question, 'You?'

He drove her home. She had never noticed before how lovely the countryside was. Green things were very green. Even the weeds in the roadside ditch. Late flowers still dotted the roadside, the hills, everywhere. A bluejay was sitting on their mailbox at the side of the road, making raucous demands of passers-by. A battered old truck was sitting next to the barn.

'Grandpa's home!' She was so pleased that she allowed Clarke to share her smile. 'My second most favourite man,' she tried to explain. 'You must stop to meet him.'

'I don't know about that,' he laughed. 'Do you suppose he would appreciate the way I've been treating his granddaughter?'

'Well, if he doesn't, you'll know about it real soon,' she laughed. 'Gramps has a tendency to be—well—outspoken, I guess is the word I want. It's an old Yankee trait. Come on up to the house.'

He trailed her up the path, laughing appreciatively at the child-woman her body displayed as her hips swayed, and her hair blew back over her ears. There was a man waiting on the porch. A tall heavy man, dressed in old but comfortable clothes. White patches of hair dotted his skull between wrinkled empty spaces. His face was weathered, and his hands big enough to serve as wrenches.

'Girl!' No need to discuss his affection. He swung her up off her tiny feet and twirled her around twice, before putting her down again and kissing her cheek.

'I missed you, Samantha.'

'I missed you, Gramps. This is Mr Clarke, Grandpa. With an e that is. Mr James Clarke.'

'Ah. Mr Clarke with an e. Are you the owner of that mangy dog that's chasing my hens?'

'*My* hens, Grandpa,' she insisted, standing back pertly from him and looking up, with her hands clasped behind her back!

'Well, did you hear that, Mr Clarke,' her grandfather roared. 'However in the world we got such a little bit of woman in our family, I'll never know. And never knows her place, that one. We'll be thankful if we ever manage to get her married off.'

'Oh, Gramps,' she sighed. 'Please. Mr Clarke thinks I'm perfectly normal. He doesn't realise yet that I'm the runt of the litter.'

'Yes, well. You'll stay for supper, Mr Clarke? And you, woman, get to the kitchen. I understand from your mother that you've been gallivanting off all hours of the day, leaving her all alone.'

'But Gramps, I had an——'

'Git!'

'Yes sir. Git, sir.'

Their eyes exchanged secret love messages as they looked at each other, and then she ducked into the house. Now we'll see what calibre of man Mr Clarke is, she told herself. He's about to be put on the griddle for sure. And as if to prove it, the last words she heard as she went into the house were, 'And just what are your intentions, Mr Clarke?'

She never did hear the answer. Vicky was in the kitchen, struggling to do something with a frozen leg of lamb, and the rest of the room looked like a disaster area. 'Grandma had a headache,' the girl explained. 'She said I was to do the lamb and she'd be back in just a minute. There's no need to hurry down there, Mom. She's got my letter with her, and she's hiding in there, crying on it.'

'I'll still go, smarty. That thing is frozen. You can't cook it until it unfreezes.'

'But we don't have time, Sam. Grandpa Ephraim's here, so supper will be at exactly five o'clock, or there'll be hell to pay, won't it?'

'There's going to be hell to pay anyway, if I hear you use that expression again, young lady. Now, put the lamb on a tray, set it in the microwave oven on *defrost*, and put the timer on thirty minutes. Right?'

'Right!'

Samantha rushed down the hall to the back room that served her mother as a bedroom. A knock on the door brought no answer, so she gently turned the knob and came part-way into the room. Her mother was sitting at the bay window, the one that held the evening sun for so much longer than the rest of the house. She held her husband's letter in her hands, but was not reading it.

'Mom?'

'Oh, it's you, Sam. Come in, dear. I was daydreaming. Did you bring Mr Clarke back with you?'

'Yes I did, dear. He's out with Gramps now, getting the third degree.'

'I know, love. I'm afraid your grandfather was a little

upset when I told him you were out with a man. Not that there's anything wrong with it, of course. It's just—well, you know how men are. Your grandfather thinks that because you're small you must also be young. Very young.'

'I don't mind, Mom. He's an old-fashioned man. I know he loves me, just so long as I don't cross his principles. What's the trouble?'

'No trouble at all, dear. I'm just having a good cry.'

'Must be a reason for it.'

'Of course there is, silly. Your—my father-in-law came back from his reunion all full of beans, and read me a lecture the like of which I've not heard in ten years or more. See, you're not the only female around here that gets ticked off, love.'

Samantha hurried across the room and dropped to her knees at her mother's side. She picked up one of the soft hands, now lying in her lap, and squeezed it. 'Did you let Grandpa pick on you? You mustn't let him get away with that. Do you want me to go and talk with him?'

'What?' Her mother's eyes gleamed through a slight film of tears. 'He'd hand you your head in a paper bag! No, dear. Your grandfather talks rough—and loud, for that matter—but the heart of him is as dear as a rose of Sharon.'

'So what did he say?'

'He told me just what I wanted to hear. He told me he would have the money for my operation in the next three weeks, and that I was to call, write, and cable your father, and tell him——'

'Tell him what?'

'That's what I'm trying to figure out—how to do it politely. You know how your grandfather talks. What he said was, "tell your damn husband to get his butt back here at once!" And you know what your father would do if I sent him that message!'

'Lord, yes, I do.' And then a pause. 'Mom? Are all men that way? Touchy—domineering?'

'Well, all the men in *your* family are, love. What are you thinking about?'

'I—well, that's the way James—Mr Clarke—is too. He's just like Grandpa. He roars at you when he's angry, and he's mostly angry. I feel like running off and hiding. Or maybe I'll buy a pair of ear plugs. What do you do when Daddy roars?'

'From long practice, love, I've learned that a man can't roar at you if you're kissing him. Is that something you might try?'

'I—I don't know about that part. I think I'd be more scared of him kissing me than I am of him roaring at me. You understand, there's nothing between us. You *do* understand that?'

'Oh yes, I understand, love.' Somehow or another the tone of her mother's voice didn't quite match the words, and Sam was having trouble sorting out the meaning. 'You had better get back to the kitchen, Samantha. By now Vicky will have wrecked half the house. And you know what will happen if supper isn't on time!'

Samantha uncoiled gracefully and scampered for the door. Before closing it behind her she stuck her head back in again. 'Ear plugs,' she announced.

'Without a doubt,' her mother returned.

She was feeling rather happy about life as she waltzed her way back to the kitchen. The lamb was defrosting, and Vicky was sitting on the high kitchen stool, licking at the remnants of the chocolate cake that had been in the cake-tin for two or three days. 'Boy, are you in trouble,' the little girl announced gravely. 'He come lookin' for you.'

'Who?'

'That Clarke fellow. The big one. Grandpa wants you. Do you like that fellow, Sam?'

'I don't know, dear. I've only known him for a little while. How could I know?'

'Well, in all the books you used to read to me, the guy fell in love with the Princess the minute he saw her.'

'Yeah, well, this is real-time, and I'm not a princess.'

'You are too! He said so!'

'He said what?'

'He stuck his head in the door and said, "tell the fairy princess that her grandfather wants her on the porch. Schnell!" What does that mean, Mom?'

'I don't know, love. How about if we have carrots and peas with the lamb?'

'I don't mind. I don't like no vegetables anyways, so it don't matter to me what you put on, cause I ain't gonna eat them anyway!'

'Sassy kid. Start peeling the carrots while I go see what's wanted.'

'Okay—there's something I forgot, Mom. Did you remember we're having a three-day Teachers' Convention next week? It's Tuesday through Thursday. So on Monday, the principal says we will have an Honours Assembly, and a band concert. You have to come, and bring him with you.'

'Whoa. Get a deep breath. Yes, I remember about the Teachers' Convention. Yes, I remember about the concert, and I do plan to come. Now, bring him who with me?'

'Him. Mr Clarke. You know!'

'Now just a darn minute, young lady. I smell a mouse in the woodpile here. I was going to persuade Grandpa Ephraim to come. Now suppose you explain to me why I should bring Mr Clarke?'

The little girl heaved a big sigh at the difficulty in explaining such relatively simple things to grown-ups. Especially mothers. 'I been a pretty good kid for weeks, haven't I? I got all those stars for accomplishment, and bein' good, and like that?'

'And?'

'Gee, you are about the most suspicious mother in town, you are.'

'I know I am. It comes from living with you for six years, young lady. What happened?'

There was another pause to martial forces. 'Mom, you know that stuck-up Ellen McCrary? She's always got her nose in the air. Well, I was telling the gang what a nice mother I got, and she came over and said her mom knew you from school days, and you never got married, and if you was my mother, that meant that I was—something. I forget the word. It couldn't of been nice, though, cause she made this terrible face, and that made me mad. I couldn't let her say those things about us, could I?' The little bowed head took a quick look up to measure her audience for effect. 'Well, I couldn't, could I?'

Oh Lord, Samantha thought. How little fibs grow into big lies! By this time next week the whole of Rochester will be talking about the 'fallen woman'. I might just as well get a scarlet 'A' and wear it on my dress, like Hawthorne's heroine did. Now what? Shall I end the whole masquerade? She tried cautiously to judge the child's thoughts.

'You know, Vicky,' she said slowly, 'I'm really your second mother. Would you want to tell your friends that, and avoid all this trouble?'

The child's face lost its smile, and one hand clawed out to snatch at Sam's. 'No!' she half-shouted. 'No. You're my real mother! I don't got no other mother. No, Sam!'

'Of course, Vicky.' She drew the child into her arms for comfort. 'So I'll be your mother forever, love,' she said. And then when the excitement had passed, 'No, you certainly couldn't let her go on saying things. So you told her she was wrong, and then you walked away? Like a little lady?'

'Well—no—not exactly.'

'Worse than that, huh?'

'Yes. Much worse than that.'

'So maybe you'd better tell me about it.'

'Do I hafta?'

'Yes, and right now. Grandpa Ephraim is waiting for me. What did you do?'

'Nothin' much, honest. Outside of I punched her in the mouth and knocked her into the flowerbed at school, I didn't do hardly nothing.'

'Hardly nothing? Is that what you call it?'

The little lip began to quiver, and the big eyes glistened. The little face, so like her own, stared up at

her, demanding support. Look at that, Sam told herself.
Give or take a few years, that's me. And what the devil
does it matter what people say? Come to think of it, I
beat up on a McCrary myself once, in that same school.
And she would have killed me if Kate hadn't stepped
in! 'No,' she sighed. 'You are right, love. It probably
was the quickest way to shut her mouth. But that
doesn't explain why I need to bring Mr Clarke with
me?'

The dark eyes sparkled again. 'I knew you wouldn't
be mad at me. I just knew it. So you don't mind at all
what I told them.'

'No, of course not. What did you tell them?'

'I told them that Mr Clarke was my father, and that
you would both come to the concert!'

The statement was still ringing in her ears as Sam
made her way, somewhat dazed, out to the front porch.
Mr Clarke is my father! I should have realised. Having
a mother was just not enough for such a possessive little
darling. So she invented a father to go with the mother
she also invented. Why not. Poor little tyke. So what do
I do now? Send her to school and make her tell all her
peers that it was all a lie? Wouldn't *that* be just the way
to break her spirit. I can't do that—so now how do I
get Mr Clarke to co-operate. Maybe if I were to write a
nice story about him, and get it in the paper? Maybe
he—maybe he wouldn't mind playing 'father' to a little
lost girl, for a limited engagement? It might be worth
the try!

Her hand fumbled with the latch on the screen door.
She pushed her way out on to the porch, breathing the
sweet moist air of the approaching evening.

'And where in the name of the twelve disciples have
you been?' her grandfather roared. The pair of them
were sitting side by side in matching rocking chairs,
swaying back and forth at matched gaits. 'Talkin's dry
work. Mr Clarke and me require a little sustenance.'

'Grandpa!' It was altogether too much. First her
mother's news, then Vicky's, and now this. 'Grandpa!
You know darn well that the beer is in the refrigerator.

And you know I'm making supper! Why can't you get your own beer!'

'Hah! Fat chance,' he roared back at her. 'I'm keeping three women in my house, and I got to get my own beer? Never a chance, little girl. Beer for the both of us. Say, Samantha, you're looking a little peaked, ain't you?' She put both hands up to her cheeks. Certainly I'm a little pale, she told herself. I'm angry! I'm surrounded by a bunch of big male chauvinists, and I'm angry! But he's my grandfather, and he's set in his ways, so there's no sense in trying to change him—not at this late date!

'No, I'm alright, Grandpa. We're having roast lamb for supper. I'll bring you your beer.'

'Well, get a wiggle on,' he directed. 'Me and Mr Clarke, we are going to take a little trip out on the property before supper.'

'Small—but shapely, that one,' she heard her grandfather comment as she went back into the house. 'And cooks like an angel. Be a lucky fellow that gets *that* girl.'

'Oh Gramps,' she moaned under her breath. 'Not with that one. Don't please peddle me to *that* wolf.'

So, after a considerable amount of extraneous pot-banging, supper finally emerged, served on her mother's second-best München Steinware, and looking as if it were fit for a king. And it is, Sam thought. Fit for two kings. She watched carefully as her grandfather sliced the roast, and then assisted in serving the rest of the vegetables. Then she sat back and listened as the men and her mother talked about the world and its worries. Her total conversation during the meal was a hissed warning to Vicky. 'Don't you dare brush those carrots off the table, young lady!'

It hardly seemed a worthwhile contribution. His dog was stretched out under the table at Vicky's side, and everything that dropped from the plate was instantly consumed. What a pair of conspirators, Sam thought. And tomorrow I'm going to get that dog clipped. She must have moved her lips or something, for the animal pulled herself up to her feet, and wandered over to Samantha's chair, where she spent the rest of her meal with her cold nose resting on Sam's knee, daring her to drop something from *her* plate. Too much, she sighed. This day has just been too much! She pushed her chair back and trailed wearily off to the kitchen. For some reason or other she had concocted a strawberry shortcake for dessert.

It was a warn night for September, and after dessert the conversation moved out on the porch, while Vicky and Samantha began the long struggle to conquer the dishes. 'I should never have made that shortcake,' she told the child, as she looked at the mountain-high pile of dirty pans and dishes. 'Never should have!' Which was just the moment that the kitchen door opened, and *he* came in.

'Best shortcake I've ever had,' he announced. 'Did you make it, Vicky?'

'Not me,' the girl laughed. 'My Mom. She made it, that's what. And you should see her embroidery!'

'Hey now, wait just a minute,' Sam snapped. 'Is this a slave market or something? I'm getting altogether fed up with all these—with—what are you doing?' The last was more of a squeal than a statement. What he was doing was gathering her up in his arms, lifting her up off the floor, and kissing her very soundly. She was totally out of breath when he restored her to her feet.

'Way to go,' Vicky chanted from the sidelines. 'Way to go, man!'

'Watch it, kid,' he threatened. 'Mind your p's and q's. You've got a nice mother there.' And then, turning back to her, 'That was just a common courtesy kiss. A thank you for a fine meal, and an extra-fine dessert. The way to a man's heart is through his stomach.'

'I'm not a surgeon,' she snapped back at him. 'If I were, I'd do a transplant on you so fast it would make your head spin.'

'You've already got it spinning,' he announced, as he whacked her gently on her bottom, and went back out to the porch.

'Well!' her eight-year-old daughter allowed. 'Ain't that something!'

'Dry the dishes,' her twenty-four-year-old mother snapped. 'Stop talking and dry the dishes!'

It was seven o'clock before order was restored in the kitchen battlefront. 'Homework?' she asked.

'Not tonight, Mom. With the Teachers' Convention coming up, all the teachers are slacking off. They don't want to give no more homework, cause if they do they have to correct it. Can I watch television?'

Sam looked up at the clock. 'Okay,' she agreed, 'but only until eight o'clock. And then its bath and bed. Hop to it.'

As the girl skipped out of the kitchen, Sam settled back on the kitchen stool and sighed. A chance to be still at last! How come I'm so young, and yet the day wears me out so easily? Maybe I ought to go into the city tomorrow, and get a check-up at that 'Walk In' Clinic out at the Mall?

Her hands swept down her dress, unconsciously smoothing it around her hips. In the mad rush to make supper she had barely managed a wash, never mind a change of clothes, and here she was, still in—as her hands moved over the soft cotton, she felt a rustling in the pocket. Dear Lord, she thought, my letter! The letter that came in yesterday's mail, and that I stuffed in my pocket this morning. And look how eager *I've* been. I haven't even opened it.

She pulled the considerably battered envelope out of her pocket. 'Editorial Department, Deltona Books,' the return address said. Great day in the morning! I've never gotten a letter before! Usually they just stick a form letter inside the envelope with the manuscript, and send the whole thing back! I don't think they really have anybody who reads the stuff. I think they have a kid in the mailroom who just rips off the outside envelope, throws in the rejection slip, and mails the thing right back! But I've got a letter! I wonder what they have to say. Nothing good, of course. Why would they. This is the sixth and last of all the publishers. I wonder what it says?

She sat there, tapping the envelope on her thumbnail. Tap, tap, tap. I wonder what it says. Well, why don't you open it, you fool! Her fingers seemed almost unable to do so. She struggled to tear off a corner without destroying the envelope. That was very important. Her first letter from a publisher. She definitely had to save the envelope! But it was beyond salvation. Her fingers, suddenly hungry for the contents, tore wildly at its container, sending little torn pieces tumbling towards the floor.

The letter was single-spaced, of course. Don't do like I do do, do like I *say* do. Editors don't have to conform to the rules! Where the devil are my glasses! On top of the stove, where else. She fumbled them on to her nose, and almost died.

'Dear Miss Clark,' the letter said. 'We have examined the manuscript of your adventure novel *The Third Kind*, and find it, with a few exceptions, to be a highly publishable tale. The difficulty lies in the sex-scenes included between pages 102–106, and 321–332.

'It is our best judgment that you are perhaps a little too inexperienced in this particular field to make the story as realistic as it might be. We would especially call your attention to the scene on page 330, which, in our editorial view, would appear to be physically impossible.

'Nevertheless, the novel has great potential. We have decided to hold your manuscript, pending further revisions. May we suggest that you consult someone with more experience, and then re-write the scenes indicated?

'May we hear from you in some haste. The market is just ripe for a story such as yours.

Sincerely.'

The signature that followed was illegible.

She held the letter up in front of her, just staring at it. She took off her glasses and held the paper out at arm's length for a second reading. Nothing in the message changed. They like it? They like it! She gave a whoop of joy, and was dancing herself around the kitchen when he came back in.

'What in the world's going on?' he asked. That baritone voice was just enough to slow her down. She faltered to a halt, and thrust the hand holding the letter behind her back.

'Hiding something?' he asked casually. 'I've got to go now, and your grandfather suggested I come in and say goodbye to you.'

'Goodbye,' she snapped, backing away from him into a corner.

'Better tell me, little Sam,' he laughed. He stalked her deeper into the corner, until her breasts were brushing against his shirt.

'No,' she snarled. 'It's private. Stop that!'

One of his hands had gone around her waist, and then dropped suggestively down the curve of her hip. Her hands moved automatically to dispossess him. And in the doing his hand came out holding the letter over his head.

'Oh—you monster! You rotten——' She tried vainly to jump high enough to recover her property, without success. And there he was, standing in the middle of *her* kitchen, reading *her* mail, with a wide wide grin on his face. I'll kick him, she told herself mutinously. I'll kick his ankle, and that will make him—that will make him mad. I don't dare to do it.

'Wonderful,' he told her, still holding the letter out of reach. 'Your first acceptance?'

'Yes, damn you,' she muttered. 'Give me back my letter.'

'But needs experience,' he continued, paying her no attention. 'That's true, Sam?'

'Don't call me Sam!' She stabbed at him with her eyes.

'And you need more sexual experience!' His laugh was as cold as a Christmas Eve in Wyoming. 'Who in the world would need more experience than you've had, Sam. You've even got a daughter to prove it to them!'

He dropped the letter on to the kitchen table, and gathered her in his arms, as if she were a package he had lost at the depot.

CHAPTER FIVE

She pondered her problem all through the long night. All you had to do was to tell him the simple truth, she lectured herself. It's easy. You look up at him and say, 'Vicky is my niece, not my daughter.' What could be more simple? And then maybe that cold look would disappear. Maybe he wouldn't kiss you so hard, so viciously, that it became a punishment. All you had to do was to speak to him. And you didn't. Why, Samatha? Why?

She knew the answer. Because it was Vicky's need. It was Vicky who introduced herself as the daughter. The girl still had a desperate need for a mother. Having her own mother walk out of the house and just disappear was too much for the child. The gap had been filled by discovering a new mother. And a break in the structure would do serious harm to the little girl. And that's why you don't tell him, Sam! After all, it's none of his business, is it? It isn't as if you were in love with him!

At that point her conscience stuck. She tossed and turned in her bed, the same one she had used since she was fourteen. His face followed her whichever way she turned. Of course it's none of his business. But wouldn't you like it to be? Wouldn't you like *him* to be your business, Samantha? How would it be if he were here right now? Practical Samantha giggled. We'd need a wider bed. Romantic Samantha shivered. How wonderful it would be! What could the book editor have meant, that the scene on page 330 was physically impossible? Huh! What do *they* know!

As a result, neither the chickens or Grandfather got fed on time, and there were the usual acrimonious words about 'leave a passel of women alone in the house for a week, and everything goes to pot!' Plus some other precise comments when he found Samantha mooning out the kitchen window 'when there's lots of womens' work to be done. Women didn't act like that in *my* day. You'd better believe it, Samantha!'

To which, being a smart aleck at heart, she had made a response just before she ducked out the back door. 'That's not true, Grandpa,' she teased. 'There *weren't* any women in your day. Why would an upstanding young man like yourself need a *woman*?'

And since all he threw after her was a chuckle, she knew that the loving humour beneath his rough exterior was still in good shape. It was a crisp clear morning, with just the tiniest hangover of early morning fog. She made her way over to the swing, hung on the old maple tree behind the house. The dog trailed along with her. Ignoring the wet seat, she pumped herself up and down, scattering the conference of robins who had reserved the tree for their own. The birds complained, and two huge blue jays came over to investigate. A clear day, she told herself. Clear weather, and a clear slate. And a story assignment in each of the next three weeks. Along with a sharp query about the next story on the Bridge.

Unusually full of energy, she slid off the swing and started over the hill behind the house, into the depths of the farm. The dog seized the new challenge happily, and went spurting off into the fields in front of her. The earth was soft beneath her sandalled feet. The corn had been harvested, leaving fields of stubble behind. In the distance she could hear the motorised harrow at work under the hand of her grandfather's hired hand. All the earth sings His glory, she hummed a line of the old hymn. Unexpected noises just over the crest of the next rolling hill attracted her. Here in the depths of the farm the flooded cranberry bogs awaited harvest. Her curious feet carried her up to the crest, with the dog dodging playfully around her.

Below, in the tiny valley, ran the little stream that would eventually become the Mattapoiset River—the Sweet Water, in the old Algonquin tongue. But directly in front of her the little brook had been damned, forming a lake of some twenty acres. Fish splashed contentedly, wild blueberry bushes crowded the shores, and an occasional white-tailed deer came down to drink. Far enough from house or road to avoid attention, deep and clear enough to swim, or sail. Silent enough to serve a little girl as her great confessional cathedral, walled in by stands of solid old pine, and a scattering of birch and oak.

And there below her, a team of surveyors were running boundary lines, their marker-poles bright in the sun, their transits busy. She stopped, frozen. 'Oh no!' The moan escaped her startled control. Transits. Running boundaries. That's how Grandfather planned to get the money. He was selling the valley! She whirled around, picked up her skirts, and ran for the farmhouse, half-a-mile away.

She was out of breath when she burst through the kitchen door, only to find the house in confusion. 'Grandpa,' she called, heedless of her mother's attempt to divert her. 'Grandpa!'

The old man was using the telephone, an instrument he hated. The farther away the caller, the louder he felt compelled to talk. And this caller must surely be a long way off! 'Three weeks from now, on Thursday,' he yelled. 'That's the best of the choices. Three weeks, Thursday. Me, I'll bring her. Don't be worried about that. How?' He was silent for a moment.

'So okay,' he yelled, 'I'll hire an ambulance. It's only sixty miles to Boston. I said I'd——' he stopped and glared at Samantha's impatient wavings. 'Wait, Sam. Can't you see I'm talking on this damn thing? Wait.' And then back to the telephone. 'Alright, Doctor Schmidt. Ten o'clock on Thursday, three weeks from now!' He slammed the telephone down in its cradle. 'And now what do *you* want, young lady?'

'Grandpa. They're down in the valley. They're surveying the valley. You wouldn't sell it?' Her eyes added a special pleading, which he brushed aside.

'Already done,' he grunted. 'Tell your Ma to come in here.'

'But Grandpa—there's acres and acres of land out

there that you don't even use. You could have sold
some of the boundary land, but not the valley!'

'I'm selling what the man was willin' to buy,' he
snorted at her. 'He wanted the valley, and I wanted the
money. Give him an easement for a road too, I did. It
brought a good price.'

The old man stood up stiffly, shaking at the arthritis
in his bones. He cuddled her against his oak-form, as he
used to do. 'Samantha,' he said gruffly, with a taste of
tears in his voice. 'Your father has no touch for the
land. A place can't be a farm without farmers. I had
hoped that Kate and her George—but, well.' He
stopped to blow his nose. 'Look at you Sam. You're
too small to farm, even if you do like farm living. Are
you planning to bring me home a farmer-husband, girl?
Charlie Aikens, maybe? He ain't much to look at, but
him and his father, they're both good farmers.'

'Oh Grandpa,' she sighed. 'I don't—I just don't
know. Of course it's your land, and you can sell what
you please.'

'Thank you, Sam.' There might have been sarcasm in
his tone, but she did not detect it. 'Now go tell your
mother to get herself in here.'

When Vicky came home at about two-forty-five, a
small celebration was in progress. The girl willingly
joined in, but her little face demonstrated that she had a
problem. When finally she managed to corner Samantha
in the hall, she hurried her difficulties out for viewing.
'Today's Friday, Mom. And Monday is the concert. Is
he coming?'

'I haven't had a chance to ask him,' Samantha
sighed. 'Come on back to the party. Grandma's going
to the hospital in three weeks for her operation. Isn't
that something?'

'Yeah—but—you will ask him?'

'Just as soon as I see him, love. Promise.'

'Well, here's your chance, Mom. He just drove up.
You go to the door. And ask him the minute he comes
in. Please?'

'Alright. The minute he comes in. Now you scoot

into the living room and tell your grandmother how much you love her!'

The bell thundered before Samantha was ready. She had not expected him. There was no time to change. Very suddenly she regretted her noon-time shift from dress to battered denims. But there was something she could do. She pulled the hair-grips out of her hair, ran her fingers through the soft plaits, and left it to hang in silken glory around her head. That's what he said he liked, and a girl asking favours has to offer something in exchange!

'I'm coming,' she yelled frantically as she managed the last ten feet to the door and threw it open.

'I like your hair,' he said immediately. He leaned against the doorjamb, looking as if he had put in a hard day's work. His jeans were mud-caked, and a ring of perspiration circled the unbuttoned cotton shirt. 'Remember me?'

'Yes,' she responded, still struggling for breath. 'You're the engineer fellow, and your name is Clarke, and Vicky thinks that you are a very nice man, and on Monday there is a band concert at her school, and she will be playing in it, and she needs a father and she wants you to. Just for Monday.'

'Let me run that back and look at it again,' he laughed. 'You are asking me to——'

'To be Vicky's father at the band concert.'

'Oh? Just for the band concert?'

'Well of course. What else did you think?'

'I'm not real sure. What happened to Charlie?'

'Charlie can't come. The cows won't wait, you know. And besides, Vicky specifically asked for you. It's only for one day, and you can be sure I won't impose on you any further.'

'And is there a mother in this act?'

'Yes. Me, of course. Who else would be her mother?'

'I'm not too sure, lady. Should I go out and come in again?'

'Well, will you?'

'It depends. Do I get all the prerogatives of a husband?'

'I don't understand. I suppose so. Will you?'

'Can I have some time to make up my mind?'

'Of course. As long as it takes for us to walk to the living room. She has to know right away so she can alert her friends. It's very important to her. And to me too, of course. And then I need to ask you something else, please?'

'Say, this really is my day,' he laughed. 'I'm not even in the door yet. Are you going to ask me to come— good lord, what is that?'

Samantha, her train of thought completely disrupted, turned around to look. 'Oh that!' she ventured. 'That's your Damn Dog. I took her in to the vet's this afternoon and had her clipped. Even without all that hair she's very big, isn't she? She must have known something terrible was going to happen to her today. Last night she wouldn't even sleep on my rug. She insisted on climbing up on my bed.'

'I knew there was some reason I hated that dog,' he said. 'Climbing on your bed is *my* act, not hers.'

'You needn't be jealous. It's not hardly big enough for me, never mind your dog.'

'Ah, but you and I could fit very easily,' he leered. She blushed. Damn the man! Every time I open my mouth he attaches some sexual connotation to what I have to say. She was just about to let her temper-balloon go up when she remembered that she was asking for favours. She summoned up all the cool she could find, and regained control. Not without sputtering, which he noticed.

'I want to ask you——'

'Are you overfeeding my dog? She was already overweight when we came here. And even with a clipping she looks as if she's gaining weight. What did the vet say?'

'He said she weighed in at 104 pounds, and she ought to weigh——'

'And how much do *you* weigh?'

'STOP IT!' She made it as loud as she could without actually screaming.

'Okay,' he chuckled. 'There's no need to be abusive.'

'No.' She gulped in two deep breaths of fresh air. 'Mr Bainsboro, at the newspaper, he wants me to do one more story about the bridge, and I can write down what I saw the other day, but I need to know what you're going to do about it. The bridge, I mean.'

'Easy,' he declared. 'I am under contract to devise something for the present bridge. I'm going to fix it.'

'And I can quote you?'

'You bet. Can I come in now?'

For the first time she suddenly realised that she had been blocking the entrance. She stepped back out of the way, almost falling over his dog as she did so. The animal gave *him* an injured look, and started to lick Samantha's hand. She followed him in, doing her best to settle her mind. Why was it, she asked herself, that every time he shows up I seem to lose control of things? For a man that I don't really like, he has a strange effect on me. Him and his dog. I've got to do something about that dog!

That afternoon proved stranger than she had anticipated. He had come, he said, to see her grandfather. The two men joined the celebration for a moment, drank beer to match the ginger-ale for the women, and then disappeared into the study. And closed the door behind them. Which was, in itself, an out-of-ordinary thing to have happen.

When they came out they were laughing over some shared joke. They're two of a kind, Samantha thought, watching them. Broad shoulders, strong faces, tall. And how can they be alike? He's got light hair, blue eyes, a dimple. Grandpa is all wrinkles and bronze. And yet they look alike!

Clarke bent over for a short and private conference with Vicky, and then walked out of the house. 'Wouldn't stay for a meal,' her grandfather commented. 'Too dirty for eating at table, he said. Fine young man, that. You paying attention, Sam?'

'Oh leave the girl alone. She's got enough troubles on her plate already.' Samantha smiled a private thank you at her mother for the quick support. That's the trouble with men, she thought. He's just a perfect match—for Grandpa. With me, it's different. All he wants from me is—well, what *does* he want from me? What a silly question ! Think back on all the conversations we've had. What he wants is a quick roll in the hay. At least I *think* that's what he wants. I wonder what he really told Grandpa the night he was asked what his intentions were? I'll bet that took a lot of fast shuffling and fancy footwork. Obviously he waltzed around the truth some. If he had come right out with it, Grandpa would have had him by the scruff of the neck. I wonder . . .?

She took her wonderings back into the kitchen, through the usual evening duties, and up to bed. 'He said yes,' Vicky whispered to her after she had said her prayers.

'That's all? Just yes?'

'That's all, Mom. He *is* nice, isn't he?'

'To little girls, he certainly is. Goodnight, love.'

She went to her own room. Grandfather was in the living room downstairs. If she went down, without a doubt there would be an inquisition. It isn't worth it, she told herself. It's not that I don't know the answers—Lord, I don't even know the questions.

The dog was still behind her, hanging close. When Samantha sat down at the typing desk, the animal flopped on the floor at her feet and rested a heavy chin on her knee. 'Well, one thing we're going to do, dog, is to get better acquainted, you and I. And the first step is that name of yours. I will *not* have an animal in my house called *Damn Dog*. No matter what he says. No matter what he roars at me. I wonder why he keeps that up? He talks to mother in a normal tone of voice, but me he has to roar at. He's not married. I wonder what he thinks about marriage. At twenty-four a girl is getting pretty old. What was that television joke? A girl who waits too long for Mr Right may end up getting left? What am I thinking of?

The dog whined at Sam's agitated movements. She rubbed the scalped head on her knee, picked up her copy of her novel, and turned to the offending pages. Physically impossible? The phrase haunted her all night long.

Saturday was clean-up day at the house. Time to wash all of Vicky's school things, to change all the sheets, to do mounds of laundry in an inadequate machine. Eventually, tired of the conditions, she piled everything into three laundry baskets and went down to the Laundromat on Route Six.

Her mother was nervously twittering around the house when she got back. The idea of *Operation* in the present tense had finally sunk in. 'It's real now because we have a date, and plans, and—your father can't get back in time, love.'

It took an hour to calm her down, and then Vicky came in with a scratched leg from playing down at the creek. All of which required more soothing. In the afternoon she abandoned the household, and drove down to Wareham with the dog, to join an animal-obedience class. 'So we still need a respectable name for you,' she told the dog as they drove back home. 'Something that will be appropriate, and will make him angry. How about—no, that won't do. We'll call you—Beauty! And let him make whatever he wants out of that!' She repeated the name so often that the dog began to believe it.

Saturday night Charlie came for her, and took her to see *Death of a Salesman* at Your Theater, in New Bedford. They shared burgers at McDonald's, and came home late.

She went to bed Sunday night tired, proud of her achievement with the dog, with her daughter, with her mother, and even with her grandfather, who had condescended to beat her four games out of five in checkers. It left a nice glow. As she dozed off, though, she recalled that the bridge story was not yet written, and it bothered her considerably. The quiet night had no answer to her problem. She drifted off to a chorus of katydid's, and the haunting call of a hunting owl.

The next day at school included ceremonies, awards,

but no actual classes, so Vicky was able to sleep late, and caught her bus at nine rather than at eight. 'He said to tell you he would come at eleven-thirty,' she whispered to Samantha before she started down to the road, music case in hand. But that still didn't mean that the chickens could be overlooked, or her mother not bathed, nor her imperial grandfather not breakfasted in royal style. Among other things. 'I think we should go back to keeping our own cows,' her grandfather announced. 'Wouldn't take no time at all for Sam to milk in the morning, and we'd save a bundle.'

'Except we couldn't get it pasteurised,' Samantha pointed out. 'And besides, I've got enough to do as it is.'

'Huh! Women. Sit around the house all day, and call it work!'

'Grandpa,' she sighed. 'I'm truly in a hurry today. Please don't tease me.'

'Me tease you?' he gruffed. 'I mean every word of it.'

She stopped her to-ing and fro-ing by his chair, and gave him a hug. 'You're a big fraud,' she announced, as if it were a new idea, instead of one she had conceived when she was nine years old. 'You and my father. Two big frauds. Now leave me be. That—that man is coming by to take me to school.'

'You mean Clarke? Takin' you to school, is he? Good idea.' And that had ended all the delaying tactics. Sam finished the last of the chores by ten o'clock, then rushed upstairs to bathe. Dress selection was no problem. She had only one 'best' dress, the kind that made it's way by understated simplicity. The *little black thing* that every woman needs in her closet. Silk. Slinky clinging silk, that smoothed down over her firm breasts, swooped in at her tiny waist, and then fell wide and swinging to her knees. A simple lace collar, and a zippered back made it just right for showing off the string of pearls her father had given her years before, when they were living high on the hog in Tokyo. A hard brushing made her hair shine in the sunlight. A touch of moisturiser, but no powder, since her tan was fading to

just the right shade of golden brown. A little eye-
shadow to emphasise those green eyes. A touch of
mascara to darken her light lashes. Too much?

'Not at all,' she told her mirror image. 'It's what
every mother would expect to do for her daughter. Go
first class. It's got nothing at all to do with that man.
Nothing at all! And if he says a word about it, I'll tell
him so in several hundred well-chosen words!'

When she came downstairs at eleven o'clock her
mother oohed appropriately, and her grandfather
nodded his approval. 'Can't catch no fish without bait,'
he commented. She wanted very desperately to tell him
that she wasn't fishing for anything, but knew that it
would only make things worse. But I'm *not*, she assured
herself as she commanded Beauty to *stay*. The dog
obeyed. Which certainly was the right way to start the
day, wasn't it?

When he came whistling up at full speed as usual, he
had a different car. One she had a hard time
recognising. He came around and held the door for her.
And if he says a word, she promised herself, I'll kill
him!

He must have known what she was thinking, for he
made not a single remark. All the way to the
Consolidated School she kept turning it over in her
mind. He hadn't said a word! Why not? Surely he can
see that I've gone to a great deal of trouble to look
nice—for my daughter. And not a word out of him!
How did I ever get tangled up with such a terrible man?
He might at least have said something like—no, that
wouldn't do. Look at his mouth twitching. Is he
laughing at me again? I'll hit him!

'Not in a Ferrari,' he interposed. 'It requires a certain
amount of dignity to ride in a Ferrari. Red is my
favourite colour. You did notice, didn't you!'

'I don't know what you're talking about,' she said, so
icily that he exaggerated his shiver. 'And you've gone
past the school turn-off. Do red cars drive better?'

He smiled broadly and made a course correction,
zooming up into the school parking lot with all the

aplomb of a world conqueror. 'Indeed they do,' he returned. 'Shall we sit here for a while and be admired?'

She stared at him, her thoughts in a jumble. Every time she looked closely, she noticed something else about him. This time it was a tiny scar, running from below his ear down into the collar of his shirt. His deep bronze colouration hid it from view most of the time, but sitting here in the car with the sun bright upon him, it was noticeable. Almost unconsciously she stretched out one tiny hand and traced its length with her finger.

'Viet Nam,' he said without prompting. 'Every generation has its wars.' A terrible longing swept over her. A need to comfort him, even though she knew he needed no comfort. Against her will, she leaned over across the driving console and dropped a feather kiss just below his ear, where the scar began.

'And now we *have* attracted an audience,' he chuckled. He vaulted out of the car, came around, and assisted her. This bucket seat was worse than the one in the Corvette. By the time she fetched up on the ground almost everything up to her pink bikini briefs was on display. He was still holding one of her hands. She used the other to smooth down her dress. For a moment her cheeks were the same rose-colour as her briefs, and she thought he was about to say something nasty about colour co-ordination.

But instead, he smiled down at her, pulled her close up against him, and rended her world with another one of those casual kisses that sent her head into a tailspin. When it was over she fell back against his arms, a boneless rag doll, struggling for breath. 'What—what was that all about,' she gasped at him.

'For the audience, of course.' He waved towards the school building, where almost every window framed a curious face. Her pink cheeks turned red.

'Let me go,' she hissed at him. 'I'm not about to be the chief attraction in your sideshow. Put me down!'

'Too late,' he chuckled. 'They've all seen the show.

We might as well be gracious about it. Two for the price of one, so to speak.'

'What in the world are you babbling about.' Anger clashed with embarrassment. 'I've never met anyone in the world who could cause me more embarrassment than you. Let me go, you——'

'Hey,' he laughed, 'I thought you were going to co-operate. If I play Daddy, I get all the prerogatives. You agreed!'

'I—I didn't mean anything like this,' she snapped. 'I'm not a public show, Mr Clarke!'

'Ah! I didn't understand the terms of the treaty. I only get to exercise my prerogatives in private, huh? Well, I can go along with that. Right after I get another sample.'

She fought against him, beating her hands on his chest, wriggling to break away from him. With no success, of course. 'If you're going to fight that much,' he complained, 'I might as well go all the way.' He had been holding her gently, with one hand on her shoulder, the other at her back. Now he shifted. The hand on her shoulder swept down just under her knees, and he caught her up completely off the ground. She kicked at him. 'The audience will think you don't like me,' he mourned. She grew still, completely embarrassed. His head moved slowly down on hers, until he was so close that he went out of focus. She closed both her eyes and prayed.

The little prayer didn't come out the way she intended. When, abruptly, in the middle of things, you find yourself switching from 'God, please make him stop,' to 'Oh my God, don't let him stop!' there has to be reason! She leaned back against the strength of his arms and cautiously opened her eyes. It didn't seem to matter that he was grinning at her like a predatory wolf. It didn't even seem to matter that his hand under her knees slipped considerably higher than was necessary. Nothing seemed to matter. She stretched up both arms around his neck, pulling his head down so that his rough cheek pressed warmly against her softness. There was no further reason to ask why. She knew. When finally he put her down, the breaking of contact left her just the tiniest bit cold, alone, rejected.

It took several minutes for her to readjust her dress and her mind. He stood there calmly, as if nothing had happened. Here I am in the aftermath of a tornado, she told herself, and he acts as if it's been a dead calm. I ought to—I—I think I shall either love him or kill him. Maybe both!

'You look as if you could murder somebody,' he contributed. He took her arm and led her into the school

'I probably could,' she returned, sounding grim warning behind the wide smile she had pasted on her face. 'That's Mrs Purdy. She's the wife of the First Selectman.' Standing at his side she could almost feel the heat as he turned on the charm, and watched the stony-faced Mrs Purdy melt away to suet pudding. She tugged at his arm. 'Down boy,' she whispered.

They two chairs near the front of the assembly room. Samantha had an odd feeling, almost of shyness, walking up the aisle with her arm in his, spreading the most preposterous lie of her entire life. And as she looked across the rows of faces that she knew, they all stared back with a mad mixture of envy, approbation, and wonder. Her only consolation was in watching the trouble he had adjusting himself to a primary-school chair.

The concert that followed would have totally destroyed a true music lover, but parents are a hardier breed. The children had been in rehearsal for only twenty days, and it showed. There was one slight anomaly. The closer it came to twelve-thirty, the official school closing time, the faster the orchestra played. But finally it was over. The school chaplain gave a blessing, the crowd eddied, and some began to find their way out.

Not more than five couples had left, however, before Vicky upset the apple-cart. Her cheeks flushed, banging her clarinet case behind her, she came running up the aisle towards them. With total abandon and a shrill voice that could be heard out in the parking lot she dropped her case and launched herself at them both, tangling herself between them as they enfolded her.

'Mommy!' she screamed in pure delight. 'Daddy!'

A very large hush fell over the entire group. Samantha tried her best to hide behind the two of them, with little luck. One hundred people in the room, she estimated to herself dolefully. Every one of them knows me or knows of me. And the one thing they all know is that I'm not married. Oh Lord. This little tidbit will be all over town by two o'clock this afternoon! Oh Lord!

'We'd better go, Vicky,' he said in a very understanding, a very kindly voice. 'Your mother has just had a shock and needs some fresh air. Or something.'

'Yes, please,' Samantha muttered. 'Or something.'

CHAPTER SIX

THE two weeks that followed left Samantha in a state of shock. School re-opened, and Vicky was happily back with her friends. Grandfather alternately moped around the farm, or spent hours comforting his daughter-in-law on her coming operation. And occasionally he looked at Samantha with a puzzled expression on his face. Once he spoke to her about it.

'I was at town meeting last night,' he said when he cornered her alone in the kitchen. 'That Purdy woman, she's at it again. Gossip. I pay it no mind myself, Sam, but a woman—well, that's different. A woman has to be more careful than a man. You understand?'

'No I don't Grandpa. What does a woman have to be so careful about?'

'About your reputation, girl. There are those in town that are saying things about you and Mr Clarke. A girl can't be too careful.'

'But I only see him around here,' she sighed. And that was surely so. Almost every weekday night, for the entire two weeks, he turned up at the farm. 'To talk to your grandfather,' he said. Or, 'I need to say something to your mother.' And the evenings would pass pleasantly. But without exception, along about nine o'clock, one or the other of them would say something about needing an early night, and 'why don't you and Samantha take a walk, Mr Clarke?'

On that first night she had gone rebelliously. He had not addressed a single word to her all night. And when they stepped out into the late September night he took her hand without asking. They wandered and argued for almost an hour. On the following nights, forewarned, Samantha slipped off to the telephone, and Charlie came immediately, like the faithful sweetheart he was. Her grandfather glared at them both as they went out, but her mother smiled.

On her late return in the middle of the week, her mother beckoned her into the downstairs bedroom and closed the door. 'I'm sure you realise what your grandfather is up to,' the older woman said softly. 'He has this thing about big being beautiful.'

'I know,' Sam sighed, 'but I don't intend to be trapped by that—that arrogant man. I don't, Mother!'

'But you do love Charlie?'

'I—Mother, I don't know that either. All I know is that I feel safe with Charlie. Safe and loved. But every time that Clarke shows up I get the feeling—I—he's a hunter, Mother.'

'I understand.' Her mother paused to gather her thoughts. 'I always said, Sam, that when it was time for you to marry I would not say a word—let you make your own choices. But I have to say something here and now, if I may?'

'Anything! You know how little I know about— men.'

'Sam, the happiest marriages are made between parties who know each other—and their families—well. You know the old saying, if you want to see your wife in thirty years, look at her mother? Well, it's the same for me. You know Charlie's father, and have for years. A kinder, more gentle man I've never known. But what do you know about Clarke?' Her daughter shrugged.

But even with that advice in mind, and her own feelings solidified Sam was drawn to the flame. She made daily trips down Route Six to watch the repair crew working on the old bridge. She dawdled across the span, hoping to see *him* at work, and received nothing for her pains but raucous horn-blowing from fellow motorists. One gang of workers were concentrating their efforts on the hydraulic system under the bridge platform itself. Others were doing electrical work in the control shack on the New Bedford side, and in the hut far above the motorway. They were all too far away to be recognisable.

On Saturday morning of the second week she went to the balloon races. It was a total flop. The mayor and six of the city councillors were at the park for the launching. 'Never lose a chance for publicity during an election year,' Samantha noted. The wind began to gust in the middle of the public speeches. It dissipated the hot air at the podium, and also along the flightline. None of the balloons could be launched. But while the race was a flop, Sam's story was not. She had discovered, quite by accident, that one of the balloons was actually city property, purchased as an advertising stunt. Her report was just cleverly sarcastic enough to make a few politicians squirm. And Mr Bainsboro called again.

'You're making a name for yourself, in a small way,' he told her. 'Refreshing. The girl with the acid pen!'

Which was in no way what Samantha was aiming for. In her rambling style, it just seemed to come out that way. It bothered her considerably, but so did other more important things, so she set the particular problem aside for a while.

That Saturday night, after all the chores were finished, she went out on to the front porch to relax. It was a cool night, but not cold. The dog went with her, as usual these days. She shrugged her shoulders into a cardigan to ward off the chill, and the big rocking chair called her. The steady up and down movement, powered by the extended toes of her right foot, served as a lullaby. The evening star was rising, almost impaled on the horns of the crescent moon. There were the usual country noises. Frogs, down the road in the swamp. Grasshoppers chirping in the deep grass. A loon, sounding miles away. Flashes of fireflies.

And then it was all disturbed by lights, as a car laboured up the road. She shook her head in dismay, debating whether to disappear or stand her ground. By the time her mind was made up it was already too late. The visitor was Charlie Aikens, dressed fit to kill Carrying flowers, no less!

I should have run, she chastised herself. Maybe it's

not too late? It was of course. Much too late. He clattered up the porch steps with a big smile on his face. 'Samantha! I'm glad I caught you free.' He handed her the bouquet.

'Why thank you Charlie,' she managed to blurt out. 'How kind of you. Were you just passing by?' By the determined look in his eye she had just taken her second strike. One more and I'm out!

'No, Samantha,' he returned solemnly. 'I came on purpose to talk to you. Something important has happened.' She gestured to a seat on the porch glider beside her chair. He ignored the suggestion, and pulled up one of the lounge chairs until he was sitting almost eye to eye with her. There was no way for her to back the rocking chair away, if she wanted to, and she was not sure she did.

Dear Charlie. When he looked at her like that, his head slightly cocked, his dark brown eyes deep in emotion, she could hardly *not* remember all the golden days they had spent together as children. All the games in which he was her white knight. All the moonlight walks, hand in hand. And stolen kisses by the score. Dear Charlie.

'Do you remember all those years we've been sweethearts, Samantha?' There was a quiver of trembling doubt in his voice, as if it had taken all his courage to come to the point.

'Yes, often,' she returned softly. 'You've been a good friend to me over a lot of years.'

'Yes, well—things are different now, Samantha. We've both grown up. Here you are burdened with a sick mother, and little Victoria too. Did you know that my father has decided to retire?'

'Oh? I knew he planned to sometime, but now it's definite?'

'Yes. At the end of the year. And that means I'm going to take over the farm. Two-hundred-and-forty acres. A prime herd of mild milk cows. A good steady income, with the main house to go with it.'

'You've invested a deal of your own work in it,' she

chipped in. 'I'm happy for you, Charlie. I know it means a lot to you to own the farm. And now you've got everything you've always wanted in life.'

'Not quite everything, Samantha.' He reached out clumsily for her hand. His face was full with his pleading, his warm eyes speared her.

'You must know that I care for you,' he stammered. Oh Lord, she told herself, its a set speech. He wrote it down and memorised it, and if I say the wrong word he'll go back to square one again. He loves you, Samantha. Don't you *dare* giggle! He paused, waiting for her to offer some statement. Not me, she told herself. After *that* introduction you don't get me to say a single word!

'You must know that I care for you,' he repeated. 'No farmer can carry on a farm by himself. I need a wife. I need you, Samantha. Will you marry me?'

There, now he's done it, she thought. There can be no turning back. Not now. Childhood is behind us forever. What can I say? The trouble is that I just haven't had the time lately to think about him—in this grown-up way. Maybe I do love him. Maybe. I like his quiet determination, and the way he honours me in every deed. His spirit—but I don't know, do I? Should it be like this, love? Quietly stealing up on you from behind on a cool September night? If I say no it would mean the end of a long fruitful friendship, and he would feel terribly rejected. Do I have that right? To reject him when I just plain don't know?

'Samantha?'

'I—I was thinking, Charles. About us. All this shouldn't have been a surprise to me, but it is. I don't know what to say, my dear. You would make any girl a fine husband—and we do know each other so well. Are you sure? It's not just habit speaking, is it? Just because we've been a couple of years, and everybody else thinks we ought to get married?

'No, there's nobody else, Samantha, and never has been. You've been my girl for years—and now I want you to be my wife. Please?'

It isn't fair, she screamed at herself. Moonlight and sweet flowers, and a fine familiar face. Contentment. That's what being married to Charles would mean. We would wander down the road of life contentedly. But with no passion. No passion.

She struggled to her feet, and pulled him up too. 'Kiss me,' she begged. His arms came around her, as familiar as a brother. His lips touched her gently, and then fiercely, as if he were branding her mouth. It was a warm kiss, moist, pleasant, comfortable. She relaxed and let her emotions run. But beyond the warmth there was nothing. When he released her she stepped back, still holding his hands.

'Charlie,' she said hesitantly. 'I just—I just don't know. I've never really thought about—marriage. Give me a little time to think?' Another set of lights swung into the farmyard from the road, and moved up beside Aikens's old Ford. Charlie looked over his shoulder nervously, not willing to put up with an interruption at this critical point.

'Of course, Samantha,' he murmured. 'Take all the time you want, but while you're thinking, will you wear my ring?'

Footsteps thumped up the stairs. Over Charlie's shoulder she could see the loom of Jim Clarke. 'What the devil is going on here,' the newcomer cracked.

'None of your business,' she snarled back at him.

'And who is this guy kissing my girl?'

'I am not your girl, Jim Clarke. I'm not. This is Charlie Aikens.'

'Ah. That Charlie. Well, friend, you've had the field to yourself for a long time, but that's all over now. The competition has arrived.'

'What is he talking about, Samantha?' Charlie was completely confused by the frontal attack. There had been some gossip—not true, of course, about Samantha and some man at the school.

'It's about you kissing my girl,' Clarke interrupted. 'Hadn't you better leave?'

It was all too much. Samantha's temper reached the

boil and overflowed. Her eyes sparked as she turned on Clarke. 'I've told you before,' she said through clenched teeth. 'I'm not your girl. I don't even like arrogant men.' She turned her back on him, and on sudden impulse offered her left hand to Aikens. 'Alright Charlie,' she said softly, 'If that's what you want, I'll wear your ring.'

'That's what I really want.' His sigh of relief was as big as a May wind. He snatched at her hand, fumbled in his pocket, and took out a small diamond ring. It sparkled in the moonlight as he slipped it over her knuckle. 'It's a little loose,' he apologised.

'Don't worry,' she assured him. 'I'll be careful of it.' She moved into his arms again, and exchanged another warm meaningless kiss. When he broke away this time he was chortling with glee.

'It's wonderful. I can't hardly believe it.' he crowed. 'How about that, Mr Clarke. Samantha and I are engaged to be married.'

'Yeah. I see.' All of a sudden Clarke's voice had gone bleak and remote. 'But don't forget about cups and lips, Charlie. Don't you have to be going?'

'Well, to tell the truth, I do. Samantha, I've got to get home and tell my mother and father. Then I've got to drive up to Worcester. I've decided to close out the insurance business and stick strictly to farming!'

'Oh—you have to go so soon?' She was beginning to come down off her angry perch, and as she did so she wondered. What have I done? If it hadn't been for that—that man—I would have put Charlie off with some mild comment. Lord, what a mess I've made of everything. 'How long will you be gone?'

'I can't tell,' he said soberly. 'Anywhere from two to four weeks. That's why I wanted to get my ring on your finger before I left! You'll be alright while I'm away?'

'I—of course I will—sweetheart.' It was hard to force out the gentle words, but she had assumed an obligation, and those were the words he had a right to hear. Charlie kissed her lightly on the cheek, and ran down the porch stairs, singing.

Clarke stood back in the shadows and watched while the other man gunned his engine, spun the wheels, and drove off into the suddenly-angry night.

'I don't know why you did that,' he groused as he moved over to her. 'Here you are *my girl*, and you go and get yourself engaged to him. It's ridiculous.'

'You've got a nerve,' she hissed at him. She glowered with so much anger that sparks leapt out of her eyes at him.

'Why's that? You *are* my girl, and I'm Vicky's father. Wasn't that the arrangement?' He said it all boldly, but somehow she got the feeling that he was no longer all that sure of himself. And it serves you right, she muttered under her breath.

'Stop talking like that,' she snapped. 'You steam up here uninvited, and make the most absurd claims!'

'Which one. That you're my girl? Or that I'm Vicky's father?'

'Grandpa just finished giving me a lecture about appearances,' she snapped. 'With my father travelling so much, and us going with him occasionally, there are all sort of reasons for people to gossip about us. I'm not your girl; you're not Vicky's father. Not ever.'

'But you asked me, and I agreed. You said I was entitled to all the rights of fatherhood, only not in public. Isn't that so?'

'No! That's not—well, maybe I said it, but I didn't mean it that way. You conned me into saying that. You don't have any rights in me at all. You hear!'

'It would be hard not to,' he said dolefully. 'You mean I drove all the way out here to enjoy my rights, and you've reneged. What would Vicky say about that?'

'Damn you!' Her lip was quivering again. He's not going to make me cry again. He's not! Her nails scraped across her palms, giving her a painful rally point. He's not going to make me cry, she shouted at herself.

'Well, I didn't have a great deal of time anyway,' he told her. 'We're having a big family reunion in Chatham this weekend. I came to invite you to come along with me, but obviously you're not in the mood.'

Again his voice had that bleak empty sound, as if he were talking without meaning. 'But as long as I've come this far, I might as well get a sample to last. Let's see now, what was it that Aikens was doing?'

His arms swept her up gently, molded her against his rock-hard muscles, and lifted her off her feet. His head moved closer, blotting out the stars. His lips butterflied across hers. The sigh came from deep within her.

CHAPTER SEVEN

THE next week brought in October. The maple leaves began their yearly change from green to gold; the oak from green to red, as all New England put on its autumnal colours. It was the week of her mother's scheduled operation, and she required more comforting, more confidence-building. And, of course, the chickens had to be fed, Grandfather's meals were required exactly on schedule, and there was always the last minute dash to get Vicky off to school. Sandwiched in between all these regular chores was a daily run down to Route Six to see what progress was being made with the bridge. Or at least that's what she told herself, doing her best to gloss over the fact that she felt something—some longing, some desire—for Jim Clarke. Her mind refused to believe what her body was telling her. It clung tenaciously to the old litany. She wore Charles' ring. She was committed to Charles. No other man must be allowed to intrude. Her mother admired her ring and congratulated her. Her grandfather grumbled and left the room. Clarke was conspicious by his absence. And Vicky seemed inordinately pleased.

In the afternoons she went out to the Obedience School with *her* dog, and suddenly it was Thursday. Grandfather turned out in coat and tie. Her mother was more upset because her husband was delayed in Beirut than she was about the operation.

'And you all behave yourselves,' was her last admonition as a cheerful aidman closed the rear door of the ambulance. Grandfather followed the ambulance in Samantha's Fiat, because 'I don't want to get stuck with no wheels. I'll call you every night. I suspect they'll be making plans to operate on Monday.'

'And you'll stay in Boston all the time?'

'I'll stay with her until your Dad shows up. And you

two babes in the woods had better behave yourselves. If you need help, you just call on Mr Clarke. A good man, that. I talked to him about looking in on you. Mind you now, behave.'

'Okay, Grandpa. Don't worry about Sam. I'll look after her.' That was Vicky's last word on the subject. They both watched the ambulance as it turned out of sight, heading for the super-highway, Route 195. And each of them tried her best to conceal the tear that lurked in an eye.

'So that leaves you and me alone, love.' Samantha hugged the little girl to her, then held her at arm's length for a check-up. Skin and bones. Growing taller by the minute, to match her giant father. George had been a basketball star in college, and had a brief try-out in professional ranks before he settled down. She'll be bigger than me almost any day now, Samantha sighed. Bigger, and more beautiful. Her hair is just a shade lighter than mine. And those big dark eyes. Oh Lord, am I growing out of date myself? Snap out of it, there's work to be done!

'Hey, the party's over.' The words were accompanied by a friendly pat on the little girl's bottom. 'Schoolday. Off you go. I can hear the bus trying to get up the hill!'

She watched and waved as the bus pulled away on its rounds, then went back to the kitchen, followed by her faithful Beauty. Another cup of coffee, more to occupy her hands than to soothe her tastebuds. Beauty flopped down on the floor, her heavy head on Samantha's shoetips.

'Where do you suppose he is?' the girl asked the dog. There was no reply. 'Come on,' she finally proposed. 'Let's walk down to the valley and see what that developer is doing to our favourite property.'

It was a slow stroll. One that they had been making almost every morning for the past two weeks. October winds were blowing in from Buzzards Bay. Cool winds, with a bit of a nip in them. Enough to require a sweater, and a windbreaker. They walked slowly, the girl occasionally throwing a stick, which the wise dog

refused to fetch. At least she's learned to *heel*, the girl
thought. And to *sit*, and *come*, and *stay*, all on
command. What more could you ask?

The trees were all turning now, impelled by the
slanting rays of the south-moving sun. The height of the
season for colour was still distant, when thousands of
New Englanders would take auto and bus tours just to
admire the turning leaves. But a start had been made,
and everything looked amazingly beautiful. The corn in
the upper section had been harvested, leaving only the
pumpkins to mature in the same fields. And the bogs
were flooded, with the cranberries almost ready to
harvest.

When they arrived at the crest of Griswold hill she
slowed her pace even further, moving up the little ridge
with all the cunning of the original owners, the
Wampanoag Indians. There was a small saddle at the
top, and a little hiding place where she could cuddle up
against the dog and see all that was to be seen.

Over the course of her spying the surveyors had long
since gone. Next a crew had come to stake out an area
on the small rise above the pond, and had piled lumber
around it in all directions. Now the frame of a house
was evident, it's roof on, frame settled, but walls and
windows still not finished. An electric generator
groaned under the load of power tools. And a hundred
yards farther on, a large house trailer was parked.
Samantha and Beauty kept a daily catalogue of the
progress, not entirely with pleasure. The plan of the
house could already be seen, and she pictured herself
decorating and furnishing it—for someone else, of
course. And that was the thought that brought her back
to reality. 'They're spoiling the valley,' she told the dog
in disgust. Beauty might have agreed, but it was hard to
tell. Her hair was already growing back so fast that
communications were sometimes difficult.

The trip back to the farmhouse was dismal. All her
troubles were piling up at the same time, Those men are
spoiling my valley! Will mother be alright? What's
holding Dad in Beirut? Where is Clarke? He's one of

those kiss and run guys. I'm *his* girl! Dear God, Charlie, come home. I need you. My old-fashioned world is crumbling at the edges, and Clarke knows it. Damn the man! Why do I go to pieces when he's near? I'm the soul of discretion and dignity—well, maybe a little bit impulsive. So why do I crack up into instant pieces when he's around? Alright, I admit it. I've been hypnotised by him. It's lust. Just plain lust for both of us. He eats little girls like me for breakfast. Maybe I'd better go to bed with him, and get it over with. And then would Charlie have me?

Safe in her kitchen again she started to work on a light supper for two, and flicked on the radio for company. News time, of course. It was always news time when you want music. News and weather. She began to pay attention in the middle of the headline story. '. . . is the first real hurricane of the season, forming just north of Puerto Rico, with interior winds of sixty-five miles an hour, moving north on a path that may take it straight up the east coast of the United States.'

Hurricane Alfred! 'Just one more little thing to worry about,' she told the dog. Who promptly demonstrated her concern by crawling under the kitchen table for a nap.

'A big help you'll be when somebody comes by to steal, rape, and pillage,' she lectured. Beauty paid not the slightest bit of attention. But it did remind Samantha that two females, living together on an isolated farm, were not the safest people in all the world. So she went into the study, unlocked the guncase, and took out her favourite double-barrelled shotgun. It was an over-and-under gun, with a maximum spread of shot, and a minimum kick. Just in case, she locked it into the front closet, then toured the house to be sure that all the windows were secured.

Friday seemed to be a day of anti-climax. The wind had dropped to a whisper, both temperature and humidity were high, and across the rim of the southern sky there were banner-trails of wind-whipped clouds.

Too high to be a bother, of course. Vicky went off to school complaining.

'I just don't feel good, Mom. It's my head. I oughta stay home from school today. Don't you think so?'

'You know the house rules,' Sam answered. 'If you've got a temperature, or you're bleeding, or you've broken something, you can stay home. Otherwise, Miss Muffet, off you go!' But she did take the girl's temperature, and checked her all over, because there had been a few cases of German measles in the area. She found nothing.

So, while her ten o'clock scholar trailed glumly off to school, Samantha stayed close to the telephone, expecting the school nurse to call. Nothing happened. And when the little girl returned home that night she was skipping happily along in company with two of her girl friends who had been invited to spend the night.

Grandfather called from Boston at nine that evening. He sounded tired. Why not, she thought. He's darn close to seventy-five years old, and still shouldering burdens he should have long since laid down. 'Everything's fine,' he reported. 'They have made all their tests, and the operation is scheduled for eight o'clock Monday morning.' He was a man of unusually short conversations on long distance, and that was all she could squeeze out of him. That afternoon she took the girls and the dog for her daily inspection of the house in the valley, and came home really down in the dumps. A telephone call from Charlie gave some temporary relief, but when she went to bed she was haunted by dreams—and it was Jim Clarke's face she saw.

Saturday morning, after a talk-filled night, Vicky went off with her two friends to spend the day at their house. Sam fed the chickens haphazardly, prodded Beauty into the truck, and drove down to take a close look at the bridge. The local radio station had made an announcement early that morning that essential repairs were complete, and that it now stood four-square, for duty, honour, and good operations!

'And I've just got to see that!' The dog seemed to

understand. Or perhaps it was just that the truck was spaciously a dog's car. A big dog's car. So they drove slowly down to Route Six, and over the Marine Park. She brought along her camera, a couple of notebooks, and plenty of pencils. The park was practically empty. The outer harbour was like a sheet of glass. Practically all the boats of the fishing fleet were tied up at the dock. The gulls had disappeared inland, as if they knew something that man did not. Packing her notebooks into her capacious bag, she whistled up the dog and started out along the sidewalk, two hundred yards or more, to where the central span of the bridge waited. A ribbon had been stretched across the roadway, and a variety of people, stalked by television cameras, were performing some ceremony.

Samantha sidled along one of the rails to get within listening distance. Beauty walked proudly along beside her, indignant growls clearing a path for them. Politicians again, she noted. Mr Prichard. While *Government* spoke over a mobile public address system, Samantha's eyes and hands were busy, noting changes in the roadway, and on its lower platform. The only thing she needed from the public speaker was his name—spelled right, of course.

Finally a ribbon was cut, a burst of applause saluted the action, and the crowd eddied away, back up the hill into New Bedford. Sam took one more look around, then, looking for a tasty quote or two, crossed the rest of the swing-span and introduced herself to Michael Souza, the bridge tender. He was proud of his bridge, and more than glad to explain the new transistorised control panel. While he was explaining, the clock winched its way up to ten o'clock, and a vessel in the outer harbour blew its horn for the bridge opening.

Samantha watched as the boat came confidently up the channel. It was the old *Lydia Schmidt*, a combination tug and workboat, about seventy feet long, known locally as *Unlucky Lydia*. It's battered bows made the reason for the nickname obvious.

And then, as she watched, the water under the stern

of the old boat erupted into a froth as she fought her
forward movement, and bucked to a stop.

'What's the matter,' Sam asked anxiously as she
turned to the bridge tender. He was standing in front of
the brand-new control panel, pushing buttons like mad,
and saying some obviously uncomplimentary words
under his breath in Portuguese. 'What's the matter,' she
repeated.

'What's the matter?' he roared at her, beating his fists
on the sides of the control panel. 'What's the matter is
that this bridge—this thing—is stuck in the closed
position!' He said some other words, some in English.
Samantha pretended that she didn't hear, and removed
herself very quickly from the area. Irate men were
always a problem for her. And irate big men especially
so. Even Beauty seemed to be walking with her tail
between her legs as they re-crossed the bridge and
reached the truck. Down-channel the *Lydia Schmidt*
was whistling like an enraged dowager, demanding the
right-of-way that Coast Guard regulations provided
her. Sam shut off her ears, pushed Beauty up into the
seat, and drove very carefully back to the farm.

Supper was left-overs. With Vicky away it didn't
seem worthwhile to make a meal. She nibbled on a
salad, managed a ham sandwich with home-made
mayonnaise, and fed the dog. Upstairs at her typewriter
she made three attempts to start the story about the
bridge, and threw them all in the wastebasket.

At six o'clock she moved over to the family room and
the television set. All three Providence stations carried a
short film on the rededication of the bridge. They
included a few statements, panned the crowd, briefly
pictured the bridge, and left it at that. Not one station
reported what had happened afterwards, and not one
mentioned Jim Clarke!

She went back to her room with dragging feet. She
had to write a story. Her work ethic required a truthful
and complete story. There was no way she could leave
out the ending, no matter whom it hurt. Warily she
started to type. After four tries she managed to concoct

a piece that had praise for the effort, and for the engineer, with a few nice words thrown in for the politicians. But then, to meet her own stringent code, she added a paragraph about the bridge malfunction.

It was later than she thought when she finished, and she had completely missed her time-slot for calling in stories. But her experienced father had told her once about deadlines. 'Better late than never,' he said. 'Let the editor worry about it.' So she placed the call.

'You know you're later than hell,' a somewhat disgruntled re-write man complained. She was all apologies as she read him her story. He said nothing more until she finished. Then a chuckle came down the wire. 'Hey,' he laughed, 'I didn't know you were the poison-pen girl. Another zinger, huh? I'll punch it up, but I don't think they'll put it in the Sunday edition. Maybe Monday, if the editor decides it's not too old.'

Poison-pen lady! That irritated her. Surely it wasn't as bad as all that? She had gone out of her way to heap praises on Clarke—on James. But all the same, as she wandered around the house there was a spot of apprehension in the back of her mind. What if he didn't like it? What if he got mad again, and never came near the house again. Ever? What difference would that make? He hadn't been near the place all week, had he? That demonstrated great devotion, hey? I suspect by now he's forgotten my name. And I'm going to forget his!

The ring of the telephone interrupted her, and her grandfather's voice trickled down the wire. 'Everything's alright up here,' he announced. 'The operation is still on for Monday, and your mother is not *too* bothered by it. I heard from your father. He plans to come to Boston, and straight to the hospital. Are you okay?'

She did her best to whip up a little enthusiasm. 'Yes, Gramps. Vicky is over at Tracy's house for an overnight party, and I'm catching up on the stories that I hadn't finished.'

'You mean you're all alone in the house?'

'Oh Grandpa! I'm twenty-four years old, for

goodness sakes. And I've got the biggest dog in the world to look after me.'

'Well—yes, I suppose that's so. Good dog, that one. Has that Clarke fellow been after you while I've been away?'

'No. I haven't seen him at all.' Her voice dropped a register, and sounded doleful even to her own ears. 'I went down to see the dedication of the bridge, after he fixed it. And I went down to the valley, Gramps. They're building a house down there. A big ranch-style house.'

'None of our business what they do down there,' he answered. 'You keep away from that place.' And he hung up.

She was halfway between laughter and tears. Good old Grandpa. Girls were made to be protected. They don't go out at night without a trusted male escort. They don't hang around where construction people work. They don't do things that will spark gossip. Their place was in the kitchen, wasn't it? Woman's work? And yes, because she loved him, she respected his opinions, and would think twice before violating his rules and regulations. With a sigh she wandered back up stairs, the dog just behind her, and tried to make sense out of the criticism of her novel.

Sunday morning was strange, weather-wise. There was a hushed expectancy about the world. High clouds—very high—fled northward at high speed. The sun was out, but it seemed weak, and there was a yellow cast to the sky. She tuned in the weather forecast as she did the pick-up work around the house. Fair to partly cloudy, the report said. Warm. Hurricane Alfred had reached full strength, with winds over 95 miles an hour. It was moving. Up the chain of the Greater Antilles, and across Cuba. There was a chance it would come north, off-shore from the American continent, missing all the big population centres. She shrugged her shoulders, snapped off the radio, and made off for church.

The exchange of children between families was made

right after Sunday school was dismissed. Vicky was full of conversation, but evidently there hadn't been a great deal of sleeping done the night before. The truck had hardly gone a block before the child closed her eyes and dozed off, her head wedged into the corner between the seat and the door. When they arrived at the house Beauty came around to meet them. But the little girl, only eight years old, was too much weight for Samantha to move, so she regretfully woke her up and helped her stumble into the house.

It was a quiet afternoon. Vicky slept through until supper time, tried her luck on a ham salad and toast, managed to yawn through a warm bath, and was back in bed by six o'clock. By that time Samantha had settled on what to wear to the Policeman's Ball. A reporter, of course, is not supposed to crash the party, or distract from the invited guests' appearance.

By the time the baby-sitter arrived, at seven, Sam was dressed fit to kill. The most stylish of all her meager wardrobe. A matched set of knee-length knickerbockers, with brass buckles just below the knee. A soft rose blouse, with white lace at the Peter Pan collar. And over-vest, knee socks, and shoes with brass buckles. Eye catching on her small full figure, not the least masculine, but so much different from the participants as to avoid comparison.

She ran through her background notes. The ball was sponsored by the Policeman's Benevolent Association, for charitable purposes. The Mayor would be present to make some awards, and then the dancing would begin. But Sam knew she need only get the names spelled right, and add a little colour. A piece of cake!

'I should be back by eleven,' she told Sally Westmont, her usual baby sitter. 'She went to bed this afternoon, and fell asleep again right after supper. I wouldn't be surprised if she has a restless night.'

'I know,' Sally responded. 'My little sister went to the same sleepover. There wasn't a deal of sleeping done.'

'Just so we both know,' Samantha laughed. 'There's

ice cream in the refrigerator, and about half an apple pie on the stove.'

She checked her notebook and camera, snatched one last sip at her coffee cup, and went out. The sky looked peculiar. One half of the dome, northward, sparkled with stars. The Dipper was hanging low on the horizon, pointing at the Pole Star. But to the south, almost as if a line had been drawn, everything was blanked out. Low clouds. The bright lights of the city, reflected a red and amber glow off the bottom of the clouds. There was a tiny movement of wind.

She spread a blanket over the seat of the truck to protect her outfit. Grandfather used it for work and pleasure, and there was no end to the dirt ground into the seat covers. She turned north this time, heading towards the express highway. For some unknown reason she felt the need to keep away from the bridge on Route Six. At a steady fifty five miles an hour, the legal speed limit, she was crowded into the right lane by cars and trucks whipping by her as if she were standing still. Her destination was only five exits away, the junction that led her back to Route Six, and into Lincoln Park.

The old amusement park, halfway between New Bedford and the neighbouring city of Fall River, was a place for family fun. The ballroom gleamed with light. She struggled around to the back, to the parking lots, then pinned on her press-pass and started the trek around to the front entrance. The night was heavy—too warm for October. Most of the participants had already arrived. Samantha took up a good position, and managed to get three good pictures of the Mayor being greeted by the President of the Association. And then inside.

The orchestra surprised her. Fifteen pieces, with strings and brasses. Not a disco outfit by any means. And the place was packed. Sam spent a few minutes getting her bearings, and finally tracked down the Chairman of the Ball Committee, and secured a guest list of celebrities. She checked over the names wearily.

That's all I do as a reporter, she told herself. Stand on the sidelines and make sure that the names were right. But it was a start. She knew how lucky she was to have *any* job at all in journalism. She could thank her father's name for that. It had opened doors.

Her list completed, she moved along one wall of the ballroom to absorb some of the flavour of it all. Shall I stay for the presentations, she asked herself. Feature one, feature all. Social life is that kind of bird. And I don't have time, she told herself.

Some of the decorations for the ballroom consisted of potted ferns. She took advantage of one of them to see but not be seen. There was a chair back there too, a spindly thing that looked like wrought iron, but threatened to collapse when she sat on it. Look at them go. A waltz. And they're dancing in an orderly circle, as people did in the old movies of Vienna. Everyone in it's—their?—place, swirling around gracefully. Long white skirts flared as partners swung their ladies sedately around. Lucky girls, Sam chuckled to herself. Every one of them with a man's arm to lean on. And look at me, trying to hide my sparkle behind a potted fern!

She stretched a little, to follow the happy faces as they came towards her in stately twirling patterns. All young, all lovely, all—my God! it was—him! Twirling one of the prettiest girls in the ballroom, moving sedately down the line towards her. James Clarke, with his curly hair sparkling in the strobe lights, his blue eyes flashing, his dimple showing—for somebody else! For just one moment she wanted to run out on to the floor and yell at him, 'Here I am! What are you doing with this—this nothing!' But of course she restrained herself.

As they passed by her sheltered seat she studied in detail the pleasure written all over the girl's face. I'd like to scratch your eyes out, she stormed to herself. You've got a nerve, stealing my man right out from under my nose! *My* man. Lord, please don't tell me that he's *her* man. I don't want to hear that. I just don't want to hear!

Almost sick to her stomach she made her way towards the door, hiding as best she could from the celebrants. A curious security guard held the door for her as she ran out under the portico that sheltered the drive. She force herself to slow down. Don't run, walk. At least until she was beyond the glare of lights, and sheltered in the welcome darkness. She stopped then to catch her breath and look back. Through the glass windows of the ballroom she could see that they were still waltzing. The pair of them, smiling at each other as if they had their own private world.

'Damn! Damn!' The tears came. She stumbled towards the parking lot, heedless of the stream of tears running down her cheeks. 'Damn! Every time I meet him I end up crying!' she moaned. She barely managed to get back to the truck. The key would not fit. She struggled with it in both hands, until finally it found the keyhole, and the door opened. She climbed in, fumbled the ignition on, and started the motor. The old truck rumbled and groaned at her. She beat on the steering wheel and answered in kind.

She jerked the truck into gear, spun it around, and made off for the highway. At the turn-off for Route 195 she stopped. The tears were blinding her. She had pulled into the far-left lane to make the turn across Route six. The light changed four times before she noticed. Two cars behind her blew their horns. To hell with it all, she told herself. She jammed the gear shift into position, and instead of turning left, went straight ahead. A speeding car behind her, assuming she would turn, veered wildly around her. She ignored it all.

The old highway meandered through the town of Dartmouth, through the city of New Bedford, and down to the bridge. Stopping on the bridge is strictly prohibited. She stopped, and rolled down her window.

Down in the harbour, lights gleamed as vessels moved. The warning light on the Hurricane Dyke blinked at her. She leaned out her window. There was a freshness to the air. All around her were the girders and guards of the bridge. His bridge. High above her head, on top of the superstructure, lights blinked to warn off low-flying aircraft. Blinked a warning.

I should have see that, she told herself bitterly as she shifted back into gear and began to move. I'm *his* girl! What a laugh that is! Stupid mixed-up woman, what did you expect? He's got a girl on every bridge in the State. This longing has got to stop. I owe all my loyalty to Charles. Why cry after lollypops I can't have? I promised Charlie I would think seriously about marrying him—and look what happens! I run around wailing after an arrogant, impossible man. Oh God, Charlie, please come home. I need you! Come home before it's too late! She shuddered as that last thought smashed home. She banged her fists impotently on the steering wheel. The bridge made no response.

CHAPTER EIGHT

SHE was up early on Monday morning, picking through the chores with one ear tuned to the telephone. It was a silent race she was conducting. Grandfather was bound to call. The operation was scheduled for eight o'clock, and Lord knows how long it will take, she told the chickens. Beauty, behind her, was evidently disappointed at the chickens' response. She growled a few times, but came to heel on command, and thrust her nose into Samantha's hand.

'Good girl,' she commented as they went back to the kitchen.

'Who me?' Vicky was trying to eat her toast standing up, half dressed.

'None of that now,' Samantha admonished. 'You'll wear a proper slip with that. You're going to school, not to a disco. And sit down properly while you eat. Don't forget your egg.'

'Boy, what a grouch you're getting to be!'

'Am I? Why—of course I am, aren't I. I'm worried, love. About your grandmother and her operation.'

'And about that man,' the little girl chuckled. 'You should see yourself, Sam. You get all wide-eyed and gooey, as if you were going to melt! Sally Parkman says you must be in love, cause that's what they do, you know.'

'No I don't know, young lady. Have you been discussing me with your friends?'

'Well, of course. How else are we gonna find out anything? Nobody tells us nothin'. You know that.'

'I'll tell you what I know, young lady,' Samantha threatened. 'One more crack like that and I'm going to whack you where it will do the most good!' The words brought a sudden frown to the child's face. 'But you won't—marry Clarke, Mommy? Please?'

122

'You don't want me to marry him? I thought you liked him.'

'Not any more, Mommy.' At her mother's raised eyebrows, the child stammered on. 'I did like him. I thought he was nice. But you remember that time you and him came to school and I called him my Daddy?'

'Yes, I remember. Right in the middle of the auditorium. So?'

'So—he said that if I ever embarrassed you like that again he was going to pound my behind. I don't need no father like that.'

'Don't worry, love,' Sam said fiercely. 'I won't let him!'

The little girl, relieved, skipped off to the bus stop. Sam looked around her messy house, went back to the kitchen, and turned on the radio.

Hurricane Alfred was still all the news. '. . . with maximum winds of 112 miles an hour,' the newsman was saying. 'Alfred is moving slowly north, on the edge of the continental shelf, just parallel to Cape Hatteras at this time. Hurricane warnings have been issued as far north as New York City, and storm warnings as far north as Bangor, Maine. Damage along the coast of the Carolinas has been slight. The storm continues to follow an oscillating track.'

She walked over to the large wall-map that her grandfather kept up as a permanent decoration. Her finger traced the coastline. On such a large-scale map local inlets and coastal variations were hardly noticeable. But if a storm were to come up along the coast, it would bang into the one great projection on the eastern shore. Cape Cod. And Rochester, Fairhaven and New Bedford all huddled together at the base of the Cape. 'Oh Lord,' she told the dog. Beauty refused to interest herself. Of all the eight commands she had thoroughly learned so far, none was, 'Oh Lord.' And then the telephone rang.

She snatched at it as if it were a lifeline. It was her grandfather. 'This costs a mint,' he grumbled. 'Long distance rates before six o'clock are terrible. The operation is over, and the doctor says it looks favourable. Your mother is in the recovery room right now. Your father arrived ten minutes ago, and I'll be home tomorrow, late. Goodbye.' Bang. The receiver clicked in her ear.

'Wow!' Samantha yelled, and did a quick two-step around the room. She tried to pick up Beauty's front paws to use her as a dancing partner, but the dog was having no part of that, and thumped out into the kitchen filled with righteous indignation. 'Well, I only wanted to dance,' she called after the big animal. 'But then, I suppose a girl can't be too careful who she dances with, can she.' Which earned her a sulky wag of the tail, and nothing more.

Samantha's exuberance carried over until noontime. With no one else to talk to, she pulled out her manuscript, and began a serious study of the scenes to be re-done. Even at second and third reading they seemed to be perfectly okay to her. 'Who do I ask—consult?' she pondered as her reflection mourned at her in the full-length mirror in the hall. Charlie? He'd tell me anything he knew, but—I doubt if he knows all that much about the subject. James Clarke? I'm sure he knows all there is to know about the subject, but I couldn't get an answer from him, I'll bet. A demonstration, yes, a simple answer, no! Vicky is right. I do get all gooey when he's around. I don't understand that. I've kissed my share of boys. One or two made it interesting too. So why do I catch on fire with James Clarke?

Her face was blush-red all through lunch, and to punish herself for aberrant thinking, she limited lunch to a leaf of iceberg lettuce, a sliced tomato, and half a cucumber. As punishment, of course. It had nothing to do with the fact that she was sticking out just a little too far in several interesting places, and that her one formal gown was just the slightest bit too tight. As if he were going to take me to a ball! Cinderella can sit in the kitchen for all he cares. Wasn't that a lovely girl he was dancing with? I hope she chokes on an olive!

To punish herself even further she gathered Beauty up after lunch, and padded across the farm with her to the valley. The house was progressing rapidly. The roof was being shingled, and wallboard closed off most of the back side. It would be a sprawling house, she could plainly see from her hilltop vantage point. Everything on one floor. But its sprawl took it in a semi-circle on the high ground on three sides of a little cove, so that all the windows on one side had lake views. Despite the fact that she plain hated the builder, whoever he was, and the owner, whoever *he* was, it was without a doubt going to be a neat good-sized cottage.

She drifted back to the house, daydreaming, and refused all of Beauty's attempts to run and romp and throw sticks. And the gist of her dreams was, 'Now, if it were my house, we would . . .'

By the time Vicky came off the school bus, Samantha had managed to dream the whole day away. And very satisfactorily, too. Her father called at three-thirty, just to re-establish contact with his daughter and grand-daughter. He reported that Sam's mother had been returned to her room, after several hours in the recovery room, and there was a favourable prognosis. Sam would have loved to talk longer with him, to ask his advice, but Vicky insisted on her turn on the telephone, and the thought of mountainous telephone bills cut off further discussion.

It started to get dark about five o'clock, which was far from normal at that time of year. The radio had begun to stutter about Hurricane alerts. Alfred had picked up speed, and it's outer ring of winds was now threatening off-shore shipping along the Georges' Banks. Samantha had a strange feeling, a sort of itch in a place which could not be scratched. She went around the house with Vicky and the dog, checking the storm shutters, the barn doors, and the chicken coops.

The two girls ate supper in silence. When the dishes were hurriedly handled, they searched through the house for the old Coleman lantern and a brace of candles. Sam filled the bath tub with cold water, just in case.

At six o'clock the storm struck. Not Hurricane Alfred, but Hurricane Clarke. They heard the squeal of tyres as a car raced up into the yard, and a hammering on the door that shook it to its old frame. 'Who the devil could that be?' Samantha sat back on the couch and hoped that Vicky would get the door.

'I don't know,' that one replied, and settled herself back in her great-grandfather's big rocking chair. The thunder struck the front door again.

'I know you're in there,' the voice roared from outside on the porch, and the door was thumbed a time or two more.

'It's him! Vicky shouted. There was no need for further identification.

And he's not too pleased about the state of the world, Sam thought as she started for the door. Do you suppose somebody has burned his bridge down? Poured treacle in his dancing shoes? For once her conscience was clear. Nevertheless, she stopped a moment before opening the door, and nervously brushed down her clean but ancient blouse. You couldn't possibly come some time when I'm all dressed up, could you, she whispered, with her head resting on the door panel. It bounced in her direction as his fist hammered it from the other side. 'Oh Lord,' she muttered, and hurried to release the spring lock. He came in, brushing her aside as if she were a loose leaf falling from a maple tree.

'Do come in,' she muttered somewhat sarcastically at his back. He kept going into the living room. She followed. 'It's always a pleasure to welcome guests.' He paid her not the slightest attention, but went over to the rocking chair and dropped a kiss on Vicky's cheek. 'Hi Vicky,' he said, as pleasantly as one could desire.

'Hello Mr Clarke,' the girl returned with chilly solemnity.

'Say, I need to talk to your mother very privately. Do you suppose you could run upstairs and watch television for a few minutes?'

'I don't think so. Why should I?'

'Victoria!' Samantha's voice crackled with electricity.

'Okay, okay. I was only foolin'. I gotta go watch
Buck Rogers in the twenty-fifth Century.' She gave
them both a very strange smile, and ran up the stairs.

'And now, you!' He had been talking in a perfectly
normal manner to the child. Now his voice changed to
a roar. She squeezed both hands over her ears.

'You don't have to shout at me,' she snapped. 'I may
be a little stupid, but I'm not deaf. Not yet, at least.' He
glared at her for a moment, and then dropped into the
chair which the child had just vacated.

'Do please sit down,' she murmured, as sweet as
saccharine.

'Don't be a smart aleck,' he roared at her. 'Now *you*
sit down. Now!' Like the crack of a whip. Samantha
had every intention of refusing, but her legs failed her.
She collapsed on to the couch, and then tried her best
to look as if it were her own idea.

He was carrying a folded newspaper in his hand. He
tossed it over into her lap. She didn't dare to look at it,
knowing that if she broke eye-contact with him,
everything in the house would go helter-skelter!

'Did you write that?' The questions at the Inquisition
might have sounded the same. She forced herself to
look down at the newspaper. The front page, no less. Of
course Monday was a slow news day anyway, but there
on the front page was her story about the re-dedication
of the bridge, and its immediate breakdown after the
ceremony. She read it slowly, following each line with
her finger, as if she were a second-grader, mouthing the
words as she went along. Somehow the story didn't
sound as nice as when she wrote it, although all the
same words were there. Somehow it seemed to say that
the brash young engineer had promised a repaired
bridge, and had got egg on his face!

'Did you write that?' Back to the roar again.

'I—well—it—they put my name on it, up here at the
top. That's quite an honour, to have a by-line on the
front page, isn't it, and I—you know I wrote it.' It came
out bitter-sweet. You *know* I wrote it. But I wrote it out
of love, and it came out like poison! You don't know

that, do you, you big—man! God, what have I done now! I can't possibly cope with two storms tonight. I just can't!

'So you did write it. Every word of it?'

'I—yes. I wrote it. Every word of it. I'm sorry. It just didn't seem to read that way when I——'

'You made a fool out of me again!'

'I——' She spluttered to a stop. Why do I sit here in my house and apologise for *my* work, she asked herself. And very deep inside of her that famous temper began to build.

'Yes. I wrote it,' she snapped. 'Is there something in particular that's wrong? You know my paper is interested in the truth, and will print a retraction if the story is wrong. Is it?'

'It isn't the individual facts,' he snapped, 'it's the tenor of the thing. You purposefully went out of your way to make me look a fool, didn't you!'

'I wouldn't have to take a very long detour to do that,' she returned angrily. 'Why don't we go over it again, together. It was true that the bridge was re-dedicated, and that the politicians announced that the repairs were complete. That's true, isn't it?'

'Yes,' he growled. 'That's true. Every word. But I told them that the work wasn't finished, and they went ahead anyway.'

'Ah,' she said maliciously. 'I looked for you to get a statement. I suppose you were out somewhere with that brunette that you took to the Ball?'

'Oho!' he roared. 'That's the way the cookie crumbles. You went to the ball! Of course. I saw your story in the society page. And that got to you, did it? And so you took it out on me in that damn paper of yours!'

'That's not true,' she snapped. 'I wrote the bridge story before I went to the ball. There is absolutely no connection!'

'Like hell there wasn't!' He was trying to stare her down. Fixing her with those blue eyes, that looked so much like blue steel now. Pinning her down, as if she were to be mounted among his collected specimens. She made a great mental effort and snapped her head away, staring down at the worn carpet, hiding herself within the cocoon of her long hair.

'Well, believe what you want to,' she replied. It was hard, very hard, to keep the little tremulo out of her voice. Her lips quivered under the pressure, and a tiny globule of tear formed in the corner of her left eye. He always makes me cry, she sighed to herself, and suited action to thought.

'And that's damn unfair,' he snapped. He lurched up from the chair and was at her side, one hand coming around her shoulder to comfort, the other pressing a big handkerchief into her clutching hand. She did her best to stem the flow, then looked up at him with a hurt expression in her eyes.

'And don't do that, either,' he snapped. 'You women are all alike. Anytime things don't go your way its tears and mournful looks. You would think we'd have learned since Adam's day, but we haven't. There's no doubt in my mind, the male is an endangered species!'

'I wasn't—I wasn't crying *at* you,' she stormed. 'I was crying *because* of you. You're a madman. I wrote the absolute truth. They said the bridge was fixed, and it broke down twenty minutes after the ceremony.'

'It didn't break down,' he roared at her. She shivered, and drew back into the depths of the couch, flinching away from his anger. He tried again, more gently. 'It didn't break down,' he said. 'There was just a little hitch. The sub-contractor wired one of the new circuits backwards. That's what happens when you have to deal with the lowest bidder sometimes. But *that's* been corrected, damn it!'

'You don't have to swear at me,' she said proudly. 'Damn you! What do you want from me!'

'My father is right,' he snarled back at her. 'There's only one way to silence a woman like you!'

'W-What?'

'Forget it. The bridge works. It works fine. They are scheduled to open it up at ten o'clock tonight, so the

Lydia Schmidt can go up the river.' He stood up and moved a couple of steps away from her. 'And you, my smart little reporter, are going to come along with me to watch that opening. And after that you're going to sit down at your little vitriol typewriter, and write a complete and unbiased story. So go get a raincoat, or whatever. We're leaving in ten minutes.'

'We are not,' she told him coolly but firmly. 'I wouldn't go out with you on a night like this if you paid me money. And besides, I've got Vicky in the house. I can't leave her alone. She's too young.'

He said several very abusive words in some foreign language. At least she hoped they were in some foreign language. If they weren't, her mind was not prepared to handle them.

'Surely your mother or your grandfather can handle the kid for a couple of hours,' he snapped.

'They don't happen to be here.' She glared at him, half afraid that she might have made a mistake by admitting she and Vicky were alone in the house.

'Holy cow, I forgot!' He slapped his forehead with one big hand. 'I forgot all about your mother's operation. And she told me all about it!'

'Well, I'm sure she'll appreciate your interest,' she said stiffly. And then, curiously, 'How could she have told you? You haven't been here all week. How come?'

'She told me on the telephone,' he snarled. 'What else!'

'You've been calling my mother on the telephone?'

'Of course. Every day this last week, until the day she left. Why? Is there some reason why not!'

'I told you before,' she said coldly. 'My father's home. He'd a lot bigger than you are. You'd better be careful about my mother, Mr Clarke. He could break you in two.'

'And as I've told you before,' he returned just as coldly, 'you haven't a single idea in your head what I'm up to, do you? I don't believe I've ever met a woman like you. Here you are, what? Thirty?'

'Twenty-four,' she admitted softly.

'Twenty-four?' She could see he didn't believe it, but he continued. 'Here you are of legal age, with an eight-year-old child, and you don't seem to know enough to find your way home after the parade. What *is* it with you, Samantha?'

'You don't have to abuse me,' she sniffled. 'I know I must seem stupid to you, but you don't——'

'Oh lord, not the waterfall again,' he groaned. 'But we are going. Surely as a journalist you feel some responsibility to tell the other side of the story.'

'Yes,' she admitted softly. 'But I can't just leave Vicky.'

'And she damn well can't come with us,' he muttered. Several other muffled words were tagged on the end of the statement. Sam did her best not to hear them.

'You've got no neighbour that could come over?' he prodded.

'Not at this short a notice, on this sort of night,' she sighed. 'But—maybe Tracy would——'

'Tracy who. Would what?'

One day, she threatened him under her breath. I trained your dog, and one fine day I'm going to take *you* to obedience school, Mr James Clarke, and teach you to let me at least finish a sentence!

'Would what,' he probed.

'Tracy lives about a half mile down the road,' she said. 'We're best friends. She has a little girl about Vicky's age, and maybe she would—maybe we could take Vicky to her house and drop her off.'

'At last you're making sense,' he snorted. 'Get your coat.'

'Now just a darn minute,' she flared up at him. 'First I have to call Tracy, and then I have to see if Vicky is willing to go. Now just sit down and shut up. I get tired of being roared at!'

He suddenly relaxed, now that she proposed to let him have his own way, she thought. He rocked for a bit in the big rocking chair, and then said something she never expected to hear.

'It's my family,' he said softly. 'Three brothers, two

sisters, four nieces—so far. If you can't be heard your opinion is never sought. So we all yell at each other. I apologise, Samantha.'

I apologise? The world is coming to an end! That isn't a hurricane out there, that's the Arch-Angel Michael, with his sword, and Gabriel with his horn! I apologise!

'Well?' he asked.

'Well? Oh. Of course. I accept your apology. I should be accustomed to it. My grandfather and my father, they both talk that way. They seem to think that the louder their argument, the more logical it must be. What was I about to do?'

'Telephone,' he suggested. 'Tracy. Can Vicky stay overnight.'

'I—just for a couple of hours,' she corrected him primly. Don't let a statement like that go unchallenged, she told herself. Look what happened at the school, when you idiotically told him he would have all the rights any father had! She stalked over to the end table, picked up the telephone, and dialled.

So finally, yes, Tracy would be glad to have Vicky. Her own little daughter was working up to a panic about the storm. Samantha was a nut to go out in this kind of weather. And why couldn't Vicky stay the night, because with the storm and all, there was bound to be no school the next day, and she (Tracy) could throw them both into bed and finally enjoy her night time soap opera, providing it didn't get cancelled by another one of those stupid football games! Samantha, having said only three or four words in the whole conversation, put down the telephone completely out of breath.

He had the Ferrari again. 'You drive,' he told Sam. 'I haven't had a minute's sleep in the past forty-eight hours.' So Vicky sat on his lap for the short trip down to Tracy's house. The little girl was looking forward to the adventure, and had no qualms at all about staying over for the night.

'But you be careful, Mom,' she whispered as she

struggled to get out of the car. 'I heard Gramps say he was some kind of wolf, or somethin'. You be careful, you hear?'

'Say, who's the mother here?' she returned affectionately. And on that light note she watched the girl struggle up to the house, and disappear inside.

She made the right moves very cautiously. The car purred, and they started off. It handled beautifully, following the wet road without strain, showing no indication of planing. The rain was falling somewhat stronger, but not overwhelmingly so. It's only for a few minutes, she told herself. Her foot slackened on the gas pedal, and the beautiful machine slowed down to twenty-five miles an hour. Now, if I can only find the windshield wipers, she whispered to herself. Perhaps it wasn't all that silent. He appeared to be asleep, but one hand reached across the console, and snapped the right switch. The blade jiggled back and forth, back and forth. Maybe he wasn't asleep? Maybe this was the time to tell him about Vicky.

'I want to tell you about my daughter,' she offered hesitantly. He made not an answer, but a tiny whistle seemed to be forming at his lips, in cadence with a sound that was suspiciously like a snore. Oh well, she sighed. Another time.

Look at me. Driving a Ferrari down a rain-swept road, with a wonderfully beautiful man beside me. He said I was his girl? Ha! She qualified her statement as she looked at him out of the corner of her eyes, if not wonderful, at least beautiful.

'Watch the damn road,' he snapped.

'Watch the damn road. Yes sir!'

'And don't get smart!'

'Me? Of course not.' Silence crowded in on them. With the windows closed the luxury car shut out the world. Back and forth, back and forth went the wiper blades. At twenty-five miles an hour the trip seemed to be taking forever, but it didn't bother him. Another car swept up behind them, acted annoyed at their speed, blinked its lights, and swept around them.

'Damn fool,' he snorted. 'An accident just looking for a place to happen. You're driving very well, Sam.'

'Don't call me Sam,' she responded automatically. But her heart was just not in it. An apology, and now a compliment! If it wasn't for that brunette on his arm at the ball, and his constant snuggling up to my mother, I could almost think that—ah, but that's impossible. But I do admit it, James Clarke, if it weren't for my promise to Charlie, I could love you. But who do you love? Whom? I wish I knew.

Up ahead, as she came down Huttleston Avenue by the ornate old high school, she could see warning lights gleaming on top of the bridge. There was not another car in sight, but the traffic lights were still working at the corner of Main Street. Not another person moved anywhere in sight, and she wished she had the nerve. But she didn't. A red light meant stop, traffic or no, so she stopped.

He opened one eye. 'Run the damn light,' he gruffed. 'We've only got ten more minutes.'

'Yes,' she said submissively. After all, it's my licence, not yours. She slammed her foot down on the gas pedal, and the car jumped like a scalded cat.

'You don't have to tear my head off,' he complained.

'No,' she said softly. He went back to sleep.

The rain was increasing now, coming in bundles, and the wind was gusting just a little higher. High enough to shake the little car, and push against its left front wheel. She applied a little more muscle to her steering, and the car's wavering stopped. The whine of the tyres changed as they moved off the surface of the causeway, and on to the metal roadway of the bridge itself. Up ahead there seemed to be some confusion. She slowed down, almost to a stop. Off to her left, in the middle of the blackness, she could see the running lights of a boat. *Unlucky Lydia*. She chuckled to herself and let the car ease slowly forward.

And then suddenly she could hear the warning hoot of the bridge siren, coupled with traffic lights, and an automatically unfolding barrier, indications that all traffic must stop because the bridge was about to open. But there was something wrong with the scenario, and for the life of her she could not understand what it was. Straight ahead of her, at some distance, she could see the barrier dropping slowly down, on the *other* side of the span. And the world ahead of her was moving. There was a tremor underfoot. Very carefully she pumped the brakes and brought the little car to a standstill. He looked to be still asleep. And then she looked behind her.

'James, she said, nudging him gently with a finger. And then, a little louder. 'Mr Clarke? Please?'

He opened an eye and smiled at her, as gentle a smile as she had ever seen. 'You've done a fine job, darling,' he said. 'It isn't easy handling a Ferrari for the first time. I wanted to be on the other side of the bridge when it opened, but—what the heck. You see how smoothly everything is going?'

'I—yes,' she said, trying to hide the little touch of panic in her voice. 'But I——'

'Samantha, you are about the most insecure girl I've ever seen.' Somehow or another he managed to lean far enough across the console between the seats to hug her, and kiss her gently. 'Better?'

And it all came swelling up to her. Darling. And a loving kiss. It had to mean something. It *had* to! The car jerked slightly underneath them.

'Set the brake,' he ordered. 'That wind is starting to pick up.' She reached down for the handbrake, but knew she could not put it off any longer.

'James,' she said.

He was searching in his pocket for something. 'Just a minute, Sam. I have to——'

'It can't wait, James,' she pleaded.

He turned and gave her his undivided attention. 'Alright,' he said, staring into her troubled green eyes and chucking her under the chin. 'So what's bothering you?'

'The bridge,' she offered, in more panic than she could handle. 'The barrier is supposed to come down in front of us, and the red lights should be staring at us, and we're supposed to stop on the fixed section until the swinging section comes back?'

'That's the drill,' he laughed.

She took a deep breath. 'Then how come,' she asked, 'the barrier is closed *behind* us, and we're sitting in the middle of the part of the span that's moving?'

CHAPTER NINE

'HOLY —— !' he said. And somewhere in the back of her mind Samantha thought—there! It wasn't a foreign language after all! It's English. Four-letter words!

He swung the door open on his side of the car, and rain splashed in. 'Where are you going?' Whatever his plan, she had a sudden fear that if he went away from her she would be lost. She could see the headlines. 'Girl Dies on Rampant Bridge!' She scrabbled at his arm with trembling fingers. He slid back into the seat.

'I'm only going to look,' he assured her. 'This is impossible. There's a deadman switch in the new system that makes it impossible for the bridge to move until the tender actually does something! Don't worry about it. We may get a little ride, but it will be over in a minute. I'm going over to the side and take a look.'

'But it's pouring rain,' she protested. 'You'll freeze.'

'Warm tropical rain,' he assured her, and opened the door again. 'I won't be away too long.'

'You're darn well right you won't,' she muttered at him as she struggled with her own door handle. 'I'm coming too. Wither thou goest, and all that.'

'That's a silly quotation,' he commented as he struggled out. She managed to disengage her own seatbelt and joined him. In thirty seconds she was soaked to the skin, and the wind was tearing at her with eager hands. 'I'm too stupid to think up good quotations,' she muttered as he came around the car and folded her into his shoulder.

'Don't tell me that,' he yelled above the wind noise. 'I know all about you. Number one in your high school class. Eleven-hundred-and twenty on your Scholastic Aptitude tests. I know it all, lady. Close your mouth. The water's leaking in.'

She snapped her jaws shut with a bang. The muscles

ached alongside her chin. Arrogant man! I know all about you! Huh! He's got a lot to learn, this one. But it was nice to lean against him for support. The wind was still gusting, whirling. Without his support, she supposed, I could be blown right off the bridge.

Under his urging they fought their way across to the far side of the span, up on to the pavement, and out to the iron rail that guarded it. The moving span had already swung out completely, and was now stopped parallel to the channel. A gap of forty feet or more separated them from the fixed section on the New Bedford side. A stick-figure of a man was waving a flashlight wildly at them. Waving and yelling. Through hollow moments in the roar of the bridge they caught a few of his words. 'Get off the bridge . . .' he was yelling.

'Sure we will,' Clarke responded in a conversational tone. 'We'll stand here until the boat goes through, and we'll jump down on her deck, and everything will be fine.'

She looked down into the black water below them. Floodlights on either side of the bridge lighted the edges of the channel brilliantly. The surface was being whipped by whirling winds, dashing mad waves against the concrete supports. It could not have been more than twenty feet down, but it looked like ten miles to her. 'I—I couldn't jump down there,' she protested weakly.

'Good lord, I'm joking,' he returned. 'Nobody's going to jump down there. We are going to stay right here until the boat goes through. Then that man over there is going to close the bridge, and we are going to drive back to Rochester to get you some dry clothes. Now, isn't that simple?'

'You don't have to explain it as if I were a baby,' she snapped at him. 'It wasn't very funny, you know. I——'

'And you don't like heights anyway, do you,' he laughed. 'I keep forgetting that!'

'Some day,' she muttered angrily.

'Some day what?'

'Some day I'm going to get to finish a sentence in a

conversation with you, Mr Clarke. How long do we
have to stand here in the rain?'

He leaned out over the rail and looked at the outer
harbour. 'They're having trouble with that tug,' he
reported. 'They can't keep her on the right heading out
there, I guess. That wind is pretty capricious. Come on.
We'll go sit in the car.'

Her feet dragged as he hurried her back to the middle
of the span. 'That's funny,' she told him, as he helped
squeeze her into the passenger seat. He went around the
hood and took over the driver's domain.

'What's funny?' he asked as he started the motor and
turned on the heater. The warm blast struck her ankles
comfortably. She unbuttoned her useless plastic
raincoat and let the heat course up her body. All her
clothes were sticking to her like a plaster, over-
emphasising her compact figure. She could tell by the
way he looked at her, what he was thinking. She needed
a diversion.

'When we stopped,' she said. 'I noticed that we were
parked by that girder with the big number 14 on it.
Now we're next to the one marked 17.'

He craned his neck to scan the pillars, then shrugged
his shoulders. 'You must have been mistaken,' he said
gently. 'In the excitement, you know.'

'I never get excited in the excitement,' she snapped.

'Stamp your foot!'

'I did,' she admitted ruefully. 'Your carpet is too
thick. I'm sure I'm right.'

'Perhaps so,' he said, sounding as if he believed not a
single word of it. With a casual movement he flicked on
the interior lights and turned to inspect her. 'You look
like a drowned rat,' he offered.

'Thanks a lot,' she mumbled. 'You look very fetching
too.' And of course that was one of the problems. *Her*
hair, thoroughly soaked, hung around her face like
loose seaweed. His curls seemed to have tightened
under the bombardment, and looked more handsome
than ever. His eyes sparkled. Her mascara was running.
The advertisements had guaranteed it wouldn't. His

loose jacket hung jauntily on him. Her light wool sweater had shrunk until it looked as if her breasts were about to break through. And that stupid dimple! Damn the man!

She huddled over in her seat, leaning against the cold metal of the car door. 'Stop staring at me,' she said indignantly.

'I'm not staring,' he chuckled. 'Just inspecting. You had better get out of those wet things, or you'll have a case of pneumonia. Slip off that sweater. The heater is going fine. Come on.' He reached over to help. She slapped at his fingers, and squeezed even further away from him. Not for the world, she told herself, am I going to let him discover that I came out without a bra. Not for the darn world!

He laughed at her confusion. 'Come on now,' he insisted. 'I can't possibly rape you in a car like this!'

'How do I know what you're really capable of?' she snarled. 'Keep your hands to yourself.'

'Okay, okay,' he returned. 'Being stuck on a bridge with you is like dating a package of frozen lobster.' She had never heard that particular disgruntled tone from him before, and it hurt. It slashed right across her stomach, upsetting everything. And he doesn't even notice, she stormed at herself. I wish I were a brunette.

He snapped on the radio. There was no music available. On every station it was the same. Hurricane Alfred, zooming up the coast, was getting closer and closer, taking a dead set for Buzzards Bay. 'Why that's us,' she stammered. 'And I left all the garbage barrels outside.'

'What in the world are you muttering about,' he snapped. 'Garbage barrels? Who cares?'

'What's with you,' she snapped. 'Didn't you ever raise a hand at home? If this is a hurricane, it will blow the garbage all over the farm. And that's hard to clean up, brother.'

'I'm not your brother,' he grumbled. 'And if this storm comes our way it might scatter that whole house of yours over the farm, never mind the garbage. Think of what a treat *that* would be to clean up. Do they have many hurricanes in this town?'

'I don't know,' she admitted. 'Two is all I've ever heard of. Nineteen thirty-eight and fifty-two. Before I was born. If you're trying to scare me, you're doing a good job of it. I want to go home!'

'Me too,' he chuckled, 'But this car won't fly. You'll have to bear with it until that boat clears the bridge. It can't be much longer. I can see their masthead lights now.'

'Why do they keep zigzagging back and forth?'

'I don't know. I'm an engineer, not a sailor. They can't seem to hold its bow in the channel. I hope to hell——'

Whatever it was he hoped, she never found out. The masthead light, which was several feet higher than the deck of the bridge, suddenly swerved wildly. There was a tremendous crack. The bridge span on which they were sitting shook. The masthead light jumped away from them. The car in which they were sitting slipped, and slid a few feet along the roadway towards its open end.

'Good God!' he roared as he struggled to open his door. 'They'll sink that tub in the channel. We'll never get off if that happens.' He jumped out into the rain again. Too fearful to stay behind, Samantha joined him in his rush to the rail. Directly below them the hull of the tough little workboat had swung to the farthest extreme of the channel, and now was coming back at them sidewise.

'Hang on,' he yelled in her ear. Both his arms came around her, pinning her to the rail. The boat below them smashed against the central support, bounced off, and all the lights on the bridge went off. She could hear the diesel engines on the boat rise to an insane roar as it's captain drove her hard to escape from sinking in the channel.

'She's going to make it,' he shouted in her ear. She peered down into the darkness, not knowing whether she cared or not. The aft lights of the tugboat flashed a couple of times, as the boat limped away from them.

'Smart man,' he roared at her. 'He's making for Travis Island. Going to beach her up there, I'll bet.'

'Well thank heavens for that,' she yelled back at him. 'Now they can close the bridge and we can go home.' He didn't seem too eager to answer. 'Can't we?'

Beneath their feet some primordial beast gave a huge sigh, and the weight of the bridge settled down a foot or two with a jarring clunk.

'Oh brother,' he said to nobody in particular. 'Back to the car, Samantha.'

'It's dark,' she complained. 'Did they break the light switch or something?'

'Or something.' The car had slipped another ten feet down the roadway under the pressure of the wind. He opened the door and crammed her in, then came around. The motor started with the first turn of the key. The blessed heater came on duty, and she relaxed in her seat. He sat up straight, pounded the wheel a couple of times, then shifted gears and backed the car up until it was in the middle of the span.

'What's that for?' she asked. 'They'll be closing the bridge in a minute, won't they?'

'The roadway is slippery,' he told her. 'We were skidding too far. I don't want my car to fall off the edge while we're waiting.' No, of course not, she muttered to herself. Me, I could slip and fall off—and probably drown for all he cares. But not his car! Oh no, not his precious car! He reached over the console in the general direction of her leg. She jumped away from him, thoroughly annoyed. 'I'm in no mood to have you feel my leg,' she scathed him.

'Well, I'm glad of that,' he retorted. 'I'm trying to turn on my Police Scanner radio. Why do you think you're so irresistible in the middle of a damn hurricane?'

'I—I'm not,' she mumbled. 'Why are you doing that?'

'Because I don't have anything better to do,' he snapped at her. 'I'm trying to find out what's going on. I wish I had a CB radio. I could call somebody.'

She could taste the sour phlegm of fear in her

mouth. Fear of the unknown. 'Why—why would we have to call anybody?' she stammered. 'Why are the lights all out?'

'It's no problem, damn it. Stop nagging at me, Sam.'

'Don't call me—oh darn you. Call me anything you like. But tell me what's the matter. Tell me!'

'Okay,' he sighed. 'I think that when that boat banged into the bridge structure, it broke the electric cable. Without electricity the hydraulic system has failed. We're stuck here until they can repair the cable—or send somebody to get us.'

She turned her back on him, stunned, and stared out the car window. On her side she was looking over the bridge and up the hill towards New Bedford. Mellville Tower, the settlement for the elderly, was lit up like a Christmas tree. So were the buildings on top of the hill. But in the downtown section all the lights were out. So maybe its a local power failure, she assured herself. And knew it could not be true. That was the moment that the wind chose to howl at them, shaking the car, sliding it back towards the open end of the bridge. On top of everything else, that was too much. She screamed and threw herself across the car console at him.

'Hey——' he exclaimed, startled. And then wrapped her up in his arms and cuddled her close. She clung to him like a lost soul, her fingers twining into his hair, her trembling cheek pressed hard against his. It was easy to draw on his strength. She could feel her panic level fall, levered out of her by the warm solid wall of him. Cautiously she moved one hand to stroke his face. It wandered up to his hairline, down across his strong nose, on to his dimple. As it straggled by the corner of his mouth he moved his head quickly and nipped at her finger. The touch shocked her back to reality.

'I—I'm terribly sorry,' she muttered as she tried to withdraw. But getting back across the console was not as easy as coming over it in fear. She could feel a bruise forming on her hip, where the lid of the ashtray had scratched her. She struggled. When he saw that she really meant it, he lifted her up like some casual bundle and sat her down again in her own bucket seat.

'And that's the last time,' he grumped. The last time for what, she yearned to ask him, but didn't dare. I don't want to know the answer, she told herself. I'm—he's mad at me. He thinks I'm trying to attack him, or something. He's bored with me. He wants that—that damn brunette! If she were here I'll bet he would be having a ball! It was all too much. Her mind boiled over.

'The last time for what?' And as soon as it was out she cringed away from him, not wanting to hear the answer.

'The last time I buy a car with a console between the seats. This thing is the pits, lady. Is that all you wanted to know?'

'I——' What she badly wanted to do was to shut up and mind her own business, but her mouth was unwilling to cooperate.

'No,' she said bleakly, 'that isn't all I want to know. Somehow her fear had disappeared, to be replaced by a stronger feeling, a massive surge of jealousy.

'So alright, lay it on me.'

'I'll bet you would be having a better time if that brunette were here with you!' And that's it, she told herself. All the cards on the table. And now if he stomps up one side of you and down the other, you've no one to blame for it but yourself!

'Ah!' He laughed softly, as if the question had already given him considerable satisfaction. 'Her name is Elaine. Nice name, isn't it.'

'Nice,' she mumbled. 'I'll bet she's a barrel of fun.' Watch it, she warned herself. Your tongue is getting very slippery all of a sudden. You really don't want to know. Why don't you casually run over to the railing of the bridge and see if you can jump the gap?

'Oh, she surely is,' he laughed. 'Young. Full of life. She was one of the hits at the Policeman's Ball.'

'I know,' she answered glumly. 'I know. I've got eyes.'

'So you did see us,' he chuckled. 'Well, let me tell you about Elaine.'

'Don't bother,' she snapped. 'I have no interest at all in hearing anything at all about Elaine. What about her?'

'Her best feature,' he said solemnly, 'is her eyes. Did you notice her eyes? No, I suppose you were too far away.'

'Well you weren't,' she snapped. 'A little bit closer and they would have arrested you for indecent assault!'

'Meoooow! Let me tell you about her eyes. They're big, for a young girl. Remarkably clear. She never wears mascara or eye-shadow.'

'Wise guy,' she muttered, fumbling in her purse for a tissue. She turned the car mirror in her own direction. And of course her mascara was running all over the place. Why me, she muttered. Why me, God? I wear mascara maybe four times a year, and look at me. She dabbed at the mess, and succeeded in making matters worse.

'That's not what I wanted to tell you,' he continued. She glared at him, wondering if there were a switch available that would turn him off. 'I don't want to hear!'

'Yes you do, lady. She has wonderfully dark deep eyes. Almost an exact copy of her mother's. Who happens to be my sister, by the way.'

'I don't want to hear,' she shouted at him. 'Your sister? She's . . .'

'Ah, you did want to hear after all.' Listen to him laugh at me, she told herself. I wish I had something to—to hit him with!

'Yes, my sister's oldest daughter. There are three others. She's ten years older than me—my sister, that is. But don't you ever tell her I told you so!'

'No, no,' she sighed, relaxing back into the softness of the contoured seat. 'Your sister. Your sister's daughter. Your niece.' She said it all softly, a dazed expression on her face. And just the slightest tinge of relief. 'Your niece.'

'Yes.' He looked very proud of himself. As if he had won first place in the *Megabucks* lottery drawing. As if he had finally given this annoying reporter a set-down that would shut her up for good. As if . . .

'Why you rotten —— man!' she hissed at him. 'All this time I've been worrying about your niece! You could have told me. Why didn't you tell me, you—you monster!'

He laughed raucously. 'Because you didn't want to know. Because you have no interest in such an arrogant man as me. Because—hell, what's the use talking to a girl like you!' He leaned across the console, and did the impossible. He picked her up and swung her back over into his lap, plumping her down with some care, so she was not impaled on the gearstick.

'What do you mean by a girl like me,' she half whispered to him. His head was closing in on her, going gently out of focus as he moved into the field of her far-sightedness. He wasn't about to answer. She closed her eyes, more relaxed that she herself believed possible. His lips ghosted over hers, came back with gentle pressure, and then wandered down to her chin, to the pulse-point in her neck, and over to her ear. His sharp teeth nibbled at her earlobe, and she found it—exciting. His free hand came around, and with one finger he traced an imaginary line from the point of her chin, down through the valley between her breasts, and farther. She shuddered at the responses that it all triggered. Responses she had never felt before, even in her wildest dreams.

A siren interrupted them. A siren from a police car that had come up on the New Bedford side of the bridge, with all its lights blinking. The Radio Scanner stopped flashing at them, and began to talk.

'Car 16 to Central. The bridge is stuck in the open position. It will have to be blocked off from both ends. All power has been cut off out here. It looks like the cable is broken. And from what I can see, there's a car trapped on the middle of the bridge. A couple of people, the bridge-tender says. A man and a woman. Over.'

'Central to Car 16, Roger. Evacuate that area. Will make arrangements with DPW to block this end, and will call State Police about the other. There's nothing we can do about the pair on the bridge. Not in this wind, and at night. Will notify Coast Guard Search and Rescue. Maybe they can do something in the morning. Weather says this storm is turning inland and going up the Connecticut River valley. There's a tree down on to a house at 136 Elm Street. Get up there and see what's needed. Over.'

'That's us!' His fingers had switched off the radio, but not before the significance of it all had sunk in. 'That's us! Do you really think—we'll have to spend the whole night out here in the middle of the bridge?'

'It does begin to look like that, love. The whole night. What say you, shall we climb up to the next floor, or would you rather sit in the car?'

'I would rather sit in the car,' she said grimly. In the back of her mind was a brilliantly clear picture of what was above their heads in the cabin. For the whole night? Grandfather would have fits. And maybe I would, too! 'And what about Vicky? She'll be missing me before too long.'

'Not hardly,' he grinned. 'I told her I was going to take you out dancing until the sun came up.'

'Hah!' It wasn't much of an answer, but it was the best she could do at the moment. She turned her attention to putting more space between them, but the contours of the bucket seat made it almost impossible.

The rain had slowed to a drizzle, and she could see lights on both sides of her now, in New Bedford and in Fairhaven. Dead ahead, the floodlights on the hurricane dyke seemed little affected by the storm. The massive steel gates, pushed together by the huge pistons behind them, had shut out the sea itself. But spray was dashing over the top of the wall, whipped up by the world-skirting wind. In back of her the lights on the highway bridge and the causeway gave a picture of a perfectly peaceful night. And at that moment, when she was twisted around to look backwards, the wind howled down on the little car, snatched at it, and pushed it protestingly down towards the open end of the bridge. It slid for about ten feet, and then came to a halt.

'That's it,' he said grimly. 'This is no place for us, lady. If you want to stay down here, that's your privilege, but I think I'll go up to the house.

'No!' She bit her lip. Raging at him would only set his heels in more deeply. He needed to be persuaded, not ordered. Lord, could anybody ever order him? 'I—I wish you wouldn't,' she heard herself say softly. Butter wouldn't melt in my mouth! Cleopatra, no less. 'It would leave me all alone, and I'm terrified enough already.' To accentuate her words, the wind banged at the car again, and it slid a few feet more down the bridge. She squealed!

'Alright, alright,' he soothed. 'We're still okay. You say you want to sit in the car? So be it. I'll just turn on the radio here for you, and——' Another gust of wind smashed at the car. The vehicle turned slowly around, and then began to slide backwards along the metal track. 'And as you can see, everything will be fine for you, love,' he continued, as if nothing untoward was happening.

'But I can't,' she pleaded. 'I can't climb that— those—I can't climb up there.' Another gust of wind. The car slipped another few feet. 'I'll go!' she gasped. 'Hurry up! I'll go!'

She was so terrified now that she pushed her door open, and scrambled out, landing on her hands and knees. The wind seized the open door, banged it a couple of times against the hood of the car, and then tore it off and sent it whirling up-river. She was too petrified to scream.

He came around the car and helped her to her feet. 'Hurry up,' he shouted in her ear. 'While we have this little lull.' He half pushed, half carried her across the roadway, across the pavement, and out to where the narrow iron stairs led upward. Everything on their section of bridge was in darkness. It probably helped.

She closed her eyes, and let him direct her hands to the rails. Then, with him closely behind her, she forced herself up the steep staircase. The wind picked and moaned at her with fingers of strength. Twice she lost her footing, and was forced to fall back against him. He kept saying something in her ears, but the sound of the storm blocked it all out. But even though she could not hear the words, the sound was an encouragement. She bent her back to the task again.

One step at a time. Get both feet secure on one riser before attempting another. Turn here, this is the mid-distance landing. One more step. And another. And there, under her hand, was the door.

'Let me do it,' he yelled in her ear. 'And when I say jump, you jump!'

Both his hands locked on the knob, he waited patiently until the wind dropped momentarily. Then, with all his muscles, he forced the door open. 'Go!' he yelled. She didn't need the command. His arm gave her a shove that sent her nose-diving across the interior of the hut, sliding on the slippery floor until her head banged up against a chair. And behind her, she could hear him muttering as he struggled to force the door closed behind them.

And then, suddenly, the door was shut. The storm was locked out. It's noise fell from a roar to a whisper. It was still there, she knew, shaking at the windows, rocking the bridge structure, but it was outside! She took a deep breath and sat up. Her hands moved automatically to her head. There was no injury. Her mass of hair had protected her. She sighed in relief, and looked around for him.

He was standing close against the forward windows, looking down and gabbling something under his breath. She struggled up to her feet. What kind of a gentleman is that, she asked herself. After he knocks me down and sends me sprawling, he goes over to the window, and doesn't even offer to help. What kind of a gentleman is that?

'Oh my God,' he groaned. She moved over to his

side, feeling the pull of aching muscles in her thigh as she forced them to move her. Looking down, she could see what attracted him. They had left the lights on in the little red Ferrari. And there it was, spinning around on the slippery road surface. Twisting, sliding, turning, until, with one mighty blast of wind, it slid to the open edge of the bridge, teetered, and fell down into the harbour channel. For just a moment they continued to see the lights as the car settled deeper into the black waters. And then it was gone.

'Oh my God,' he groaned again. She could feel the bitterness of gall and wormwood settle in her stomach. He couldn't come to help me because he had to mourn his damn car. Is that all I'm worth? Damn the man.

'It's only a car,' she snapped at him. 'Give or take twenty-thousand dollars, what the hell!'

'Don't be flip,' he glared at her. 'It isn't the money. That was *my* car. My favourite car! A man comes to love very few cars in his lifetime, lady, and that one was my first love!'

So I had to ask, she stormed at herself. I knew it all the time. Men fall in love with peculiar things. Their automobiles, their aeroplanes—anything fast. And like a fool I had to ask! What I really need, if I intend to survive this night, is a great big—extra big—bandaid. Big enough to slap across my entire mouth, that's what!

He was fumbling around in the darkness. She edged a little bit away from him. Until the back of her knees ran into the couch. Home sweet home, she told herself. She instructed all her muscles to stand down, and dropped gratefully into the softness. And she gave another big sigh.

'What's that in honour of?'

'I—I found a place to sit down,' she explained softly. 'I—I needed a place to—oh!' The exclamation was because he had found the gas lantern. He pumped it two or three strokes, flashed a match, and lit it. Immediately the room was filled with its sharp white light. Seeing another dimension added to her feelings of safety. 'That's wonderful,' she sighed. 'You really are——' and she forced her mouth to stop. Only an idiot would let him know how much she depended on him. Only a glaring stupid idiot! Look where we are!

As if to emphasise just where they were, the wind climbed up out of its pit and rattled the bridge as if it meant to tear it away. Like an insane bear out there, teasing us, lunging at the bars of our cage, ready to eat us up, Goldilocks! It was too much. Tears came in floods. Tears of terrors unknown, thoughts unthought.

He set the lamp down on the desk against the far wall and came to her. 'Now, now,' he murmured into her hair as he pulled her close in his embrace. 'Cry away. It can't get in at us. This old bridge could stand up to a hundred storms this size. Cry it all away.'

It did seem warmer, there in his arms. The wind *did* seem to be slacking off. He *did* sound as if he could master it all. And very suddenly a chill chased up and down her spine. Responsibility! She had promised Charlie. It would have to be some other girl who spent the rest of her years with Jim. Some other girl. The phrase was like a knife to her heart.

'That's better,' he told her gently. He picked her up in both arms, hugged her, then gently stretched her out on the couch. She sighed again, a reflex action. He smiled down at her, and then turned away. Under the counter, where he had found the lantern, his fingers turned up a little propane camping stove, with a full canister attached. Moments later he had water boiling, and shortly after that, two cups of instant coffee.

'No milk,' he apologised as he brought it over. 'There may be some of that powdered stuff somewhere?'

'No. Don't bother,' she answered, smiling at him as she cradled the mug in her hands, gathering its heat. She sipped at the coffee, and again smiled her thanks. He did the same, standing over her, casting a long shadow in the light of the lantern.

'Now that isn't so bad, is it?'

'No,' she laughed. Her courage was returning with every tick of her wristwatch. Which now said half past midnight! Outside she could actually see the wind, outlined by the water-spray it carried. Twice there were large pieces of something—metal, perhaps—picked up by the wind and whirled in their direction. She flinched automatically, and then had enough strength to laugh at herself.

'That's the way to go,' he chuckled. 'Get that coffee down you. There's a can of soup on the shelf. I'll get it ready. There are more than enough blankets to go around, so while I'm getting the soup, you slip into a blanket.'

He turned his back on her, leaving her totally confused. 'I don't understand—James.' How nice that name tasted. 'I don't understand what you mean, about getting into a blanket.'

He was shaking his head as he turned back in her direction. 'Never one for taking hints, are you Sam. We're both soaking wet, girl. If we stay in these clothes, we're liable to come down with something. So, Samantha, you are now required to strip off all those wet things, and get yourself into a dry blanket.'

'You—you mean, undress? Right here? With you? All alone, with you?'

'That's what I mean, love. I don't intend to have to explain to your grandfather why I brought his favourite girl back home with pneumonia. You *are* his favourite girl, aren't you?'

'I—I guess so. But I—I can't just—do that. Not while you're here.'

'So what do you expect me to do. Climb out into the storm, and get myself drowned, just to protect your modesty?'

'But I can't do that. I just can't!'

'Okay,' he chuckled. 'You had your chance. Just a minute.' He found a can opener, and was pouring the soup into a pan set on top of the stove. When he finished he looked over the whole set-up with a careful eye. 'Worst thing in the world,' he said casually, 'is to have a fire burn your house down in one of these monstrous storms. Now then, where was I? Oh, yes. Undress Samantha.' He flexed both hands in front of him, and moved in her direction. She scrambled back into the depths of the couch. 'No you don't, you—monster,' she screamed at him. But he kept coming anyway.

Almost as if he were dealing with a little kitten, his two hands closed on her shoulders, then shifted to the hem of her sweater. 'Don't you dare!' she shouted at him.

'Wrong words, Sam. I dare most anything.' And before she could offer another object, the sweater and the T-shirt beneath it, came up and whipped over her head, leaving her sitting in a yoga position, nude from the waist up.

'No,' she yelled at him as her two hands tried vainly to cover her breasts.

'Lovely,' he commented. 'Absolutely lovely. But I knew you would be, Samantha darling.'

'No,' she pleaded, more softly. 'I'll do it myself. I'd rather do it myself.'

'Spoilsport,' he returned. 'Well, if you're sure. I don't mind finishing the job?'

'No—no. I can do it, if you—if you turn your back. Please?'

He grinned at her. A great big face-shattering grin that emphasised that hynotising dimple, and showed a cavern full of gleaming white teeth. 'Okay. Two minutes. No more.' He turned his back and started counting.

CHAPTER TEN

'SOUP's ready,' he called to her. 'But you have to finish your coffee. We've only got those two mugs available.' She smiled weakly up at him. It really wasn't so bad, was it, she asked herself. Embarrassing, of course, but not too bad. The blanket, wound around her like a sarong, covered everything from neck to ankle. Neat. All I need now is a blue ribbon with a bow, and I'll be a Christmas package. I wonder what he would like for Christmas? Me? To cover her confusion, her sudden blush, she gulped at the coffee and finished it.

He immediately took the mug and refilled it with hot soup. She clutched at it. It was too hot to drink. The wind had come up again, and the rain had changed from drizzle to cloudburst. Some of it seemed to be coming right through the glass windows. 'It's leaking around the frames,' he said. 'I think they'll hold. I wish——' he was fumbling around in the storage box by the door. 'Just the things,' he exclaimed. He had found a pair of men's socks. 'Slip into them love. The floor will get pretty cold before this night is out.'

She accepted them gratefully, sliding along the floor to demonstrate. It did help. Her feet were already chilled. He watched her as she adjusted them, showing them off in the bright white light of the lamp. 'And now,' she said, 'how about you?'

'How about me what?'

'You're just as wet as I was. Pneumonia germs don't discriminate between sexes. There are plenty more blankets.'

He watched her over the rim of his mug, and the gleam in his eye sparked her.

'What happened to Samantha the Prude?'

'Don't you talk to me like that,' she snapped.

154

'Nobody's a prude in a life-and-death situation. Even me. Get yourself out of those wet things.'

'And if I don't you'll do it for me?' He laughed as she spluttered in indignation. 'Okay, you talked me into it. But remember, I'm only doing this because you ordered it!' She watched, fascinated, as his hand moved to the buttons of his shirt and he stripped it off. Look at those muscles, she told herself in awe! For the first time she could compare the width of his shoulders, the flat plane of his stomach, all slimming down to narrow waist and hips. Apollo Belvedere? Somewhere in National Geographic magazine she remembered seeing a statue like this. But not in white marble. He was bronze, from neck to waist. No wonder he could handle me so easily in the car.

'Do you have to stare?' he asked, with almost the same intonations she had used a few minutes before. There was a teasing tone behind the words.

'Oh!' She had just come to her senses. 'No, of course not!' She ducked her head away. Out of the corner of her eyes she could see him turn his back to her, and unable to resist the compulsion, she looked again as his pants came off. Look at that, she thought. He must sunbathe in the raw. No marks or lines anywhere—Save for a line going down from just below his waist and on to the swell of his buttocks. Another scar! She stared at it, mesmerised. He started to turn towards her again, and she ducked her head. Close your eyes, she yelled at herself. Don't panic. You've seen a man undress before. Harry Curtis, remember? Of course he was only seven years old at the time, but—well, it counts all the same, doesn't it? By the time she had made up her mind he was enveloped in a blanket, and the subject didn't seem important any more.

'You look like an Indian chief,' she said shyly.

'A blond Indian? You look like a twelve year old. Drink your soup.'

As usual when with him, conversation failed her. There didn't seem to be another thing to say. She picked up the mug, cradling it in both hands, treasuring the warmth. He was doing the same, but looking around as he drank the soup.

'What the devil is that?' It didn't sound as if he expected her to answer, but she felt compelled to say *something*.

'That what?'

'That!' He pointed across the room to the little table set next to the couch. In the darkness Samantha could see nothing. He took four steps across the room, and picked up a little box. Damn!' he exulted. 'A radio. I hope the batteries are still working.'

They were. Immediately the storm appeared to recede, as voices and music from a hundred outside places invaded their tiny prison. It sounded as if the room had expanded, as if the world had not forgotten them. He turned the dials and found waltz music from a station in Canada. He offered a hand. 'Shall we dance, madame?'

She took his hand dazedly. He pulled her to her feet, and into his arms. She struggled to keep a distance from him, but his grip was too strong. Gradually, as they fell under the sway of the beat, their feet began to move, shuffling around the centre of the tiny clear space, hardly noticing the bumps as furniture was knocked about. So close. So warm. So safe. Until suddenly she realised that they were not dancing at all, but swaying gently back and forth, locked together by his arms and her fears.

Her fears! Her arms were stretched to the full, clutching at the sides of his neck, unable to reach all the way around. Clutching desperately. And that was her fear. That she might never be able to let go. That the wonder of it all would overwhelm her, tear her away from the safe shore that Charlie represented, and toss her into the ocean of this man's wild passion.

'Samantha?' he stopped moving entirely, and bent his head over to touch the top of hers. 'Samantha Clark, this is one hell of a place to say it, but I want you.'

She heard the words echo in her empty head, round and round. I want you. I want you. And once again her clever little tongue served her well. 'Oh!' it returned.

Even your own dim mind can recognise that's one terrible response, she told herself fiercely. Say something more! Be charming! But try as she might she could not squeeze out another word. Her eyes widened and tried to flash him a message. Which he was obviously not receiving. He untangled her hands and set her down a foot or two away from him. 'Oh?' he mused. 'Not exactly the enthusiasm I had expected. But then, I knew it was the wrong time and the wrong place. Let's get some sleep.' His tone had changed from warmth to chill. As cold as the iceberg that sank the Titanic!

She slumped, her shoulders drooping, her chin falling, and—here we go again, she thought. It wasn't rain running down her cheeks, but rather tears. Every time, she cried to herself. Tears. Before this affair is over, I shall have cried an ocean of tears over him.

'This couch is big enough for both of us,' he said casually. He picked up more blankets from the storage chest, and spread them out. 'A little crowded, maybe, but the squeeze will keep us warm. You take the inside.'

'I—no,' she muttered. 'I—I don't—I'm not going to sleep with you. Not me!'

'I mean *sleep*, Samantha. You know, close the eyes and become unconscious. Not that stupid word you novelists use because you don't dare to come out with four-letter words. Queen Victoria really ruined the English language when she set about to clean it up. Sleep. As in lullaby baby.'

'I don't care what you call it,' she snapped at him. This whole mess has gone far enough. First the argument, then the storm, then the car, and now this— sleep. 'Not on your life. There's a couch, and here's a chair. You can have the chair.'

His fingers snatched at her wrist as she tried to get by him. 'Not on *your* life, lady,' he chuckled. 'If you don't want to sleep with me on this couch, that's okay with me. But I'm going to sleep on the couch. If you want the chair, just go help yourself.'

She watched sullenly as he spread himself out on the couch and pulled the blankets over him. 'What kind of a gentleman are you?' she half-sobbed at him.

'None at all,' he returned. 'My grandfather was a hod-carrier. We've made a lot of money, and come up a ways, but there's still hod-carriers blood in us all. Good night.' And then he had the nerve to roll over on his side and turn his back on her! Sam seethed. Well, two can play at that game. I'll show him. Why did I think he was a wonderful man? He's arrogant, domineering, ungentlemanly, and—I'll show him!

She stomped over to the fragile chair and set it up close to the table. It was hard to get comfortable. The chair creaked every time she moved, and the table was cold when she managed to get her feet up on it. And the wind howled. She squirmed. He had shut off the propane stove, so there was little heat. The lantern glared coldly at her. She squirmed some more. There were noises coming from the couch. Listen to that. He doesn't snore—he whistles. He's not perfect after all! How would it be to be married to somebody like that!

Just barely aware of what she was thinking, a drowsy smile flickered across her face. And the wind howled. Howled and shook the hut, as if it really meant to get in. It snapped her wide awake. 'I need something,' she muttered. The radio. She snapped it on and fiddled for a local station. '. . . and hurricane Alfred has stormed ashore at the mouth of the Connecticut river, and is moving slowly up the river valley, losing strength as it progresses. And now an item of local interest. New Bedford police report that the Fairhaven bridge is jammed in the open position, trapping an unknown couple on the movable span. There appears to be no present danger. The Coast Guard is readying plans to rescue the couple at first light. Local area winds, on the fringe of the storm, have now dropped to sixty miles an hour. Police and emergency crews are standing by, but residents are asked to remain in their homes. All schools and businesses in the metropolitan area will be closed tomorrow. Please remain in your homes. And now, we bring you the Carpenters.'

'Turn the thing off,' he muttered from the comfort of the couch. She didn't mean to do it, but her fingers automatically obeyed his command. 'Lily-livered,' she muttered at herself, and tried once again to get comfortable. Every squirm brought a squeak of protest from the chair until, shortly after two o'clock in the morning, it collapsed, dumping her on to floor. She squatted there, more angry than injured. Just one giggle, she told herself. Just one laugh, and I'll murder him. I'll kill him dead!

If he did make a noise, it was masked by a sudden massive onslaught of wind that rattled the entire hut. A piece of flying debris, snatched up in the outer harbour, battered at the corner of the little building, like Satan demanding admission.

'Oh my God,' she muttered, utterly overset by this last assault. Look at me! I'm scared three quarters to death, I'm cold, I'm miserable, and I'm tired! And there *he* is, snoring away in the lap of luxury!

Very suddenly things seemed to assume a new proportion. *He's* responsible for it all! For me being trapped here, for the storm. He's responsible. We haven't had a hurricane here in over thirty years, until he came. Damn the man! He's responsible for me being cold, and tired, and scared green. *Him!*

Angrily she staggered to her feet and stomped over to the couch. She stared down at him, looking for a place to hit. He snuggled deeper into the blankets. Damn the man! She flipped back the blankets and plopped herself down beside him. Somehow or another the blankets fell in place over her, and he shifted on his side to make room. The instant warmth of him and his blankets swept up around her comfortingly. The winds outside howled in derision. She ducked her head under the blankets and found herself resting hard up against him.

Something felt strange. She was lying on her left side, facing outwards. He was lying on his left side, close up against her back. The fingers on one of her hands wandered. Somehow or another he had lost his covering blanket, and her fingers found only male flesh. Warm pulsing male flesh. She snapped her hands away.

It's very hard to lie rigidly still, and at the same time relax. The warmth, the touch of him, all conspired against her. As her eyelids grew heavy, and finally closed, she could feel him move to a more comfortable position. His right arm came up over her shoulder, and his hand dangled dangerously close to her breast. Oh what the heck, she told herself as she dropped off.

It was hard to tell what woke her up. A noise, perhaps. Or a change in the wind? But whatever, she snapped back suddenly. There was a glow of light coming through the windows, a sort of peace offering from the dawn. Not quite dawn, of course, not yet. The wind was still whistling a gale, the hut was still shaking, but that was not what had awakened her. Very slowly she searched her senses. Her hand wandered down her own leg and thigh. No blanket! Somewhere in the tossing and turning during the night she had lost the blanket she had been using as a dress. As he had too. And now he was stretched up tightly against her, flesh on flesh, and his massive hand was cupping her breast, toying with its proud bronze peak, teasing.

As she gasped, held her breath, his hand abandoned its teasing and swept down to her waist, down to where no one had ever touched before, sliding, probing, exciting. For a tense moment she made no protest. It was like nothing she had ever felt before. The hand moved up again, trailing a fiery finger across her stomach, marching up the mountain of her breast again, and poising triumphantly on the crest. Then down again to her waist, where it paused. She shivered, unable to control her emotions. And then his hand at her waist pulled her hard back against his aroused male strength, and the shock of it finally penetrated the wall around her mind. She squeaked in protest, broke loose, fell on the floor, and was running before her feet were flat in position. *He doesn't love me*, her mind screamed!

'What in the world,' he grated. But by that time she

had reached the door, palmed the knob, and pulled. It was enough, just enough, for her real enemy, the storm, to get at her. The gusting winds snatched at the partially open door and slammed it back against her, catching her just on the forehead above her eyes. Her feet, still encased in the over-sized socks, slipped on the floor, and she went hurtling back across the room until she slammed into the storage chest. She saw the movement, heard the wind, and then nothing else.

He was off the couch by the time the wind seized the door, but not in time to stop what happened. He half-stumbled over her prone body, and put his shoulder to the door. It was a battle he had to win. And he did. When the latch clicked he jammed the bolt home, and turned to her. She was lying gracefully on her side, one foot extended, the other curled slightly under her, her hair a storm-tossed mass across her forehead.

'Sam?' He dropped to both knees beside her, gently checking her neck and shoulders before he uncovered her face. The bruise had already swollen into a large blue lump. 'Oh my God, Sam, don't die on me!' His practiced hands swept gently up and down the rest of her body, looking for breaks, and found nothing.

He picked her up in his arms and carried her over to the couch, kicking the blankets out of the way as he laid her down. Gradually her eyes fluttered, and she slept.

When he was sure of her condition he stretched his cramped muscles and worked his way back into his clothes. Not entirely dry, he noticed, and yet not really wet. A sort of clammy in-between. Samantha's dress was still soaked, as were her sweater and her briefs. No use, he decided, If I try to dress her she'll wake up. And she needs the sleep. Lord, look at her. Like a great big rag doll. Beautiful. She looks a perfect innocent, despite her eight-year-old daughter. I need to protect her—for as long as forever is. God, to think I may have found her after Aikens had already stolen the prize. Should I try some other approach? It's terribly hard to wear the mask of confidence when I'm shaking at the idea that she really loves him—damn him! Maybe I should have handled her more gently? She doesn't come from a big brash family like mine. Flowers and candy and dances, if it isn't too late? I've *got* to get her to marry me. I've *got* to. There won't be another woman like her come along in a thousand years! And the little girl is giving me the cold shoulder, too. No Vicky, no Sam. That's obvious!

His musings were cut short by the sound of silence. The wind had stopped, and the rain had pattered away. There definitely was a gleam across the harbour. Not pure sunshine, but a glancing yellow that promised, if not fulfilled. He rushed to the windows and looked down the bay. The wild chopping waves had gone. The world looked clean-swept.

To his left, on the Fairhaven side, there was some obvious damage. A few yachts, not yet taken out of the water, had broken their moorings and were piled up indiscriminately on the rocks at Crow Island, and the Marine Park. At the dock on the New Bedford side there was a bustle around the stern of the Coast Guard Cutter Bibb. A whaleboat was launched, and began its way across the harbour towards the bridge.

He went back to the couch, carefully wrapped Sam in two blankets, heaved her up to his shoulder in a fireman's life, and carried her slowly down the iron stairs to where rescue was promised. She opened her eyes at the head of the stairs, raised her head slightly, then said, 'Nice,' very drowsily.

'You bet,' he chuckled. 'Now, we have to do this right, or I'll lose my licence for carrying girls. Not a wiggle out of you, Sam. You've got a slight concussion, I think.'

'Of course,' she muttered. 'The birds are singing.'

They weren't of course, but he agreed anyway, and went on as if he were carrying the most valuable of all the world's prizes. He gave her up regrettably to the two husky young coast guardsmen who were waiting.

CHAPTER ELEVEN

IT turned out to be a strange hospital stay. Although her head felt slightly wobbly, nothing else bothered her as long as she kept still. They installed her in a semi-private room in the Women's Ward, and the other bed was empty. 'Rest,' the doctor instructed, in a gruff voice that indicated she was only a minor inconvenience in a flood of casualties. So she rested for about twenty minutes before the Charge Nurse came storming down the hall with fire in her eyes.

'This—man—keeps calling on the telephone.' She glared at Samantha as if it were all her fault. 'Four times, from Providence.'

'I don't understand,' Samantha stammered, perplexed in the face of such righteous indignation. 'Why doesn't he call me here? I've got a telephone by the bed.'

'Because we don't allow incoming calls to patients,' she was instructed. 'The telephone is there in case you want to call out. This is his number, should you care to call him!' The very pitch of her voice indicated that officialdom would consider it to be only slightly possible that she might want to make the call. 'After all, you're here to rest, not to make long-distance calls.'

And that was just enough to pull Samantha out of her daze, to make the call just for spite. The number, of course, was the Providence Gazette Assignment desk, and Donohue answered. She barely had time to mention her name before he was off.

'We've been scooped, Clark,' he roared down the line at her. 'Where have you been? The *Globe* and the *Journal* both have the tail-end of a real human-interest story. A man and a woman, trapped on that bridge of yours during the hurricane. Neither of them have the whole story. They couldn't even get the names. Now get out and find us something. Hop to it!'

'I—I can't,' she yelled back at him. The movement jarred her head, and she regretted it instantly. 'I can't, Donahue,' she repeated much more softly. 'I'm in St Lukes Hospital with a concussion. There's no way I can go out on a story. Besides——'

'What the hell, Clark,' he roared at her. 'A story is more important than whatever you're in the hospital for.'

'Mr Donahue,' she said hesitantly, thinking of all her troubles, 'If I moved to Providence, do you suppose I could get a regular job with the *Gazette*?'

'Ah, well,' he laughed. 'It would depend on this story, wouldn't it? Of course you could. You're well-thought-of in these parts.'

'I can't go out,' she sighed, 'but how about an interview with the girl. Would that help?'

'I can't send a reporter all that distance at this time of day. We're up to our necks over here!'

'How about a telephone interview?'

'Yeah—well, okay. That doesn't sound too bad. What number do I call, and how can I be sure she'll talk to me?'

'She's talking to you now,' she sighed. 'Start off with the first question.'

Thirty minutes later, when the floor nurse returned with her pills, she was just wrapping it up. She put the telephone down, and wiped her perspiring hands on the towel suspended by her head. The young nurse, a Licenced Practical Nurse, bustled around her, sorting things out. 'The Charge Nurse told me to remind you that long-distance telephone calls all go on the bill.'

'Oh my,' Samantha wailed, 'I didn't think of that. Or of any bills at all. I don't have Blue Cross.'

'Why worry,' the LPN laughed. 'I heard the argument today when they brought you up. Your husband has had it all put on his account.'

'My—oh. Him.'

'Yes. Where did you ever come up with such a tasty morsel as that one?'

What does one say? He's not my husband? He's rather handsome but not mine? I'm not his wife, I'm his mistress? Or I wish I was. Either one. Nothing fit, so instead she managed, 'Oh, I found him hanging around a bridge one day.'

'You're a lucky one,' the nurse laughed, half-way out the door already. 'I only play poker.'

'I've got to learn that game, Samantha told herself two hours later. If ever there was a girl needing a poker-face, I'm it. James had come, bringing Vicky along with him. And she was terribly afraid that her glowing face might tell him more than she wanted him to know. But in the face of the child's exuberant greetings, all her plans fell by the wayside. Vicky ran across the room and threw herself on Samantha's shoulder. 'Mama!' she squealed, accompanying the words with a hug that rocked Sam's head.

'Whoa baby,' she pleaded, feeling instant nausea. 'Mommy's head is still too loose. They had to take it off and readjust it, and it takes a while to settle down.'

The child was all regrets, mixed in with happy tears. 'I thought you was gone,' she sobbed. 'They told me you went away, like—you wouldn't do that, would you Sam?'

'I promised, didn't I, love. All those years ago. No, I'll never go away, Vicky. Not until you're really grown up. There now. Satisfied?'

'Yes.' And then, with the quick-change of youth, 'We got the rest of the week off school. You know what that hurricane did? It blowed the corner off the school roof, and all the water came in on the floor and went all over Mrs Almeida's books, and they shut everything down. How about that?'

'How about that indeed. Who's taking care of you?'

'Him.' She pointed glumly over her shoulder. 'But Grandpa Ephraim is coming home tonight, and he talked to me on the telephone this afternoon and he says that Grandma is very well, and they fixed her legs good and she'll be home in three weeks, and your daddy is going to stay with her in Boston until she's ready to come home. And Beauty misses you. Ain't that something?'

'That certainly is something,' she sighed, pulling the child over for another hug. 'Everything seems to be turning up roses. Except for your bridge, James?'

He made no effort to get close, but stood behind Vicky with his hands on the girl's shoulders. The child moved away. 'It's not too bad,' he said wryly. 'I'm *glad* you're hospitalised. I'd hate to read another story tomorrow about the boy-wonder of engineering, who got stuck on his own bridge!'

Oh brother! She caught herself just in time, from saying several of those interesting words she had heard him use in the past few days. They would print that interview tomorrow, for sure. And what *would* it sound like? Valiant Gazette Reporter Rides Bridge? Or maybe Bridge Captures Engineer? Or some such stupid thing! She smiled weakly at him, and did her best to change the subject.

'Is the bridge damaged?'

'Yes and no,' he returned. 'It will be stuck in the open position until they get a new cable installed—probably by tomorrow. And then, it depends whether or not the storm warped anything. I found out how we got stuck, by the way. The new transistorised controls again. The bridge tender pushed the button marked *Siren*, but that button had been wired to the activation circuits, so that was open sesame with a vengeance. That's what happens these days. How would you like to be riding a rocket ship to the moon, knowing that some of it had been built by the lowest possible bidder on the contract? Well, we can forget it. I have. I made my recommendations, and the bridge is no longer my responsibility.'

'And—and now what are you going to do?' Don't let him know that it matters all that much, her mind screamed at her. Don't let him know! He *wants* me. Why couldn't he love me?

'I'm not sure yet. I'll probably stay in this area for a time. Pop thinks we should expand into the Cape area. And you? What are you going to be doing?'

'Oh, I don't know. Be a home nurse for Mother, of course, until she really gets on her feet. And then, who knows what Vicky and I might do.' Is this cool enough? Am I giving him the *disinterested* Samantha? If we don't get too close, he can't hurt me so much. 'I do want to thank you for all your kindnesses—and the hospital bill. I'll have to pay you back when I get a job. You won't forget to tell me how much it costs?'

'Damn it, Samantha, you don't have to pay me back. It's my fault that you're in the hospital. You make this all sound as if we were saying goodbye, or something.'

She tried to see him clearly, but the room was dim, and he was keeping his distance. So that does it, she told herself grimly. What did you expect? We had our fun time, he lost his first love—that car of his—and now its over. Probably I bruised his male ego a couple of times too many. But oh if things could have been different!

'I—perhaps I'm a little tired,' she stammered, and immediately bit her tongue. He took the statement to heart.

'Sure, they told us we could only come in for a minute. Come on, Vicky. It's time we got you home. Your Great-grandfather will be waiting for you.'

An hour later she opened her eyes at some small noise, and stared directly into Charlie's solemn eyes. A nurse hovered anxiously beside him. 'He said he was your fiancé,' she explained.

'Yes,' Sam managed hoarsely. 'Hi Charlie. You were gone so long.'

'Yes, wasn't I,' he returned bitterly. He flipped a copy of the local newspaper over on to the bed. She could barely focus on the headlines: *Nude Girl Rescued From Bridge!*

'Oh my,' she sighed.

'It's true, is it?' he snapped.

She was too tired to argue. Her long debate was finished—somewhere on the cold heights of the bridge. A barrier had dropped between the golden days of childhood and the harsh realities of maturity. And

Charlie had been left behind the barrier, on the far side. They could never be the same again. 'Yes, it's true,' she sighed.

'You realise then that you and I are finished, Samantha?' There was gall and wormwood in the words, and she would have done almost anything to spare him the pain. Anything except marry him. Not that. Slowly she tugged his ring off her finger and silently handed it back to him. He took it without a word, and left.

On Wednesday morning, the first real sunny day after the storm, her grandfather came for her. She could tell that something was wrong as soon as he came in the door.

He was as big as ever, stern, craggy, and looking like one of the Old Testament patriarchs. He had no intention of discussing his problem with her. He brought some clothes for her return trip, walked beside her wheel chair as the nurse took her to the door, and crammed her into the Fiat without a word.

They took the long route home, around through the town of Acushnet, at the head of the river. 'That bridge is still stuck,' he said, and that was his entire budget of news.

'How's Mother,' she asked as she walked gingerly into the house. The old man grunted. No, she thought, not another man who needs humouring. It must be that all men come out of the same mould. 'Well,' she continued, 'I'm tired from the trip. I think I'll go lie down.'

'You do that,' he grumbled, and turned away.

'I don't understand you today,' she said wistfully.

'You don't understand nothing, Miss. But I'll get it all straightened out. Don't worry about it. I already talked to your Mama. You go rest.'

'Talked to Mama about what?'

'That's my business. I'll tell you all you need to know when the time comes. Right now, go get your rest.'

It would take too much energy to argue, energy that she just didn't have. 'Alright Grandpa,' she said, and slowly made her way upstairs, supported on either side by the dog and the girl. Fifteen minutes later, more comfortable in her own nightie and her own bed, she relaxed against the pillows. Vicky tiptoed out, but Beauty remained, her big shaggy head resting on the side of the bed. Samantha ran her fingers through the dog's mat of hair, and closed her eyes, just for a second.

A hand rattled her shoulder. She opened her eyes slowly. 'Vicky?'

'It's six o'clock, Mommy. Grandpa Ephraim said to wake you up cause there's somebody coming.'

'Oh my. Did I really fall asleep?' She stretched like a cat. A bobcat. Short limbs and sharp teeth, and a smile for her daughter.

'You betcha. All afternoon. I come by and looked four times, but you was still fast asleep. And Beauty too.'

'And Beauty too?' Samantha sat up and looked down on the rug, where the dog was still sleeping. 'Oh well, I suppose she needs her nap. Did you have supper?'

'Yes, but Grampa didn't like it. He said he wasn't gonna eat out of no cans. But we did, anyway. Beans and frankfurters. I saved you some.'

'You are a love. First stop, bathroom. Second stop, kitchen. You go ahead.'

Her headache had finally gone, and she felt almost real. Her mirror reflected wide shadowed eyes, and a pale face, but a splash of cold water did make some improvement. She brushed her hair until it shone, putting it up in one loose braid, and carefully avoiding the bruised area that was now a sickly yellow and green. Her dress was crumpled. She made a quick change into a blue polka-dot A-line. It accentuated her youth, if nothing else.

Downstairs in the kitchen Vicky was standing by the table, where a place-setting for one had been laid. The beans should have been Boston style, baked in molasses. Instead they were canned, in a weak tomato sauce. The frankfurts should have been robust German sausages. Instead they were skinny things, fresh out of the freezer, boasting on their sides that they contained only forty-five per cent chicken. But she was hungry, and sat down to do justice to what there was. The doorbell rang just as she finished.

'I'll see who that is, Vicky. Can you get the dishes?'

'Alright, Mom. Did you 'joy the meal?'

'As good as steak and champagne,' she laughed, and wandered carefully towards the door. Twilight had already set in. There were stars sparkling around the outline of the man on the doorsill. She was startled, and a little pleased. 'James?'

He came in, brushing by her and then turning to look back. She longed to be touched, but he kept his hands at his sides. There was a sombre look on his face, as if he were facing two equally unpalatable choices.

She gestured him into the living room. 'I really didn't expect you to come calling tonight.' Somehow she barely managed to get her voice working right.

'You didn't expect me? That's a laugh. I read all about myself in the *Gazette* again this morning. What's with you, Samantha? Why do you always have to stick the knife in me and then twist it? Now the poor stupid engineer is trapped on a bridge which is running amok, and is rescued by the valiant *Gazette* girl-wonder. What's with you?'

'I—I didn't mean it to come out that way.' Her eyes pleaded with him for understanding. 'I—oh, James, if I could only tell you—I . . .' She swallowed her tears and cleared her throat. 'You won't have to worry any more. I'm moving to Providence to work on the paper. And I won't write about you. Please, don't be angry with me.'

'I'm not angry,' he sighed. 'But you can't move away. I'm just trying to understand. We could be good together, we two. I just don't understand why we always end up at dagger-points.

'I—is that what you came to tell me, James. Goodbye?'

'Goodbye? Where did you get that crazy idea? I came because your grandfather invited me. And he didn't make it sound like a social occasion. What does he want?'

'I don't know. I've been napping all afternoon.'

'Samantha!' It was her grandfather at his best, a roar strong enough to rock the house. 'Is that young man out there!'

'Yes, Grandpa,' she called back.

'Bring him into my study!' She shrugged her shoulders expressively at James, and led him down the hall. As he went into the study her grandfather roared again. 'And now you get that little Miss upstairs, and you wait in the living room. You hear me?'

'How could I help but,' she sighed. 'What's going on?'

'That's for me to know,' he came back at her angrily. 'And don't forget. Get that child upstairs.'

'Oh, Lord,' she muttered under her breath. 'The wild bull—and loose in the china closet!' But obedience was ingrained. She stopped long enough in the kitchen to chase Vicky upstairs, then went back to the living room and dropped on to the couch. She could hear the rise and fall of conversation from the study, but could not distinguish the words. For over a half-hour it went on, and then stopped. She heard the clink of glasses, a silence, and then the door opened. The two big men walked into the living room to where she was waiting. Very quickly she felt shrunken, like a Lilliputian set afoot in Times Square. Both men studied her as if she were an exhibit at the museum. Two big arrogant men.

'What is it,' she asked hesitantly.

'It's alright,' her grandfather said softly. 'He's going to marry you!'

CHAPTER TWELVE

'HE'S going to marry me? Who? Who said?' For an instant Samantha had the feeling that her grandfather had finally lost his mind. But the expression on the old man's face gave pause to the thought.

'I said,' he returned. 'I've talked it over with your mother and there's nothing else to be done.'

'I—I don't understand. Why does something have to be done? What are you talking about?'

'I'm talking about this!' He pushed a folded newspaper in front of her. The local New Bedford newspaper. In the middle of the front page was a picture of the Coast Guard unloading the Stokes litter at Pier Three. The litter containing blanket-wrapped Samantha Clark. The story failed to identify her, but did carry a brief sketch of their night on the bridge, told from the bridge tender's viewpoint.

'But what has that to do with anything?' she asked frantically.

'Samantha. Look at me and tell me the truth. Is that you there, in that litter thing?'

'Yes. Of course it is.'

'And just what are you wearing underneath those blankets?'

'I——'

'Don't lie to me, Samantha!'

Very suddenly she felt some sort of noose dropping over her head. Some kind of pressure, never experienced before. When else had her grandfather ever thought she might lie to him?

She stood up, trying to gain some little advantage of height. 'I've never lied to you, Grandpa. I wasn't wearing anything under the blankets.'

'And who wrapped you up in those blankets?'

'James did. But you——'

'Just answer the questions, Samantha. You spent the night alone with this man, on top of that bridge, and during the night you took off all your clothes?'

'Because they were wet, Grandpa. So I wouldn't catch pneumonia. It was——'

'You didn't think you might catch something worse than pneumonia from taking your clothes off?'

'I—Grandpa! What in God's world are you thinking? We were being practical. You must know that! And——'

'And then you climbed into bed with this man, both of you being naked?'

'Yes, damn it! Yes!' The inquisition had gone too far. Her long-suffering temper had taken all it could manage, even from a man as much-loved as her grandfather. 'But nothing happened! Nothing at all! What do you think this is, the eighteenth century?'

'Don't be smart, girl,' he growled. 'People don't change. Eighteenth century or twentieth, people are still the same. Don't tell me nothing happened. I know better. He confessed to the whole thing!'

'He what? You what?' She turned her cold angry eyes on James. He held up both placating hands. 'There's no use fighting it, Sam,' he insisted. 'He knows all about it.'

'All about what?' If only he could have said he loved me, she thought. I'd jump at marriage. But he doesn't. He loved his car, perhaps his dog. But me, he just *wants* me. I can't possibly marry him. Not now, not any time. It would be easier to say goodbye—make a clean surgical break, and see if I survive!

'He knows everything that happened on the bridge!'

'Nothing happened on the bridge,' she screamed at both of them. 'The two of you are mad. Mad! Nothing happened on the bridge. Tell him, James!'

'I can't lie,' he returned. And she knew he was lying up to his eyeballs. But why? Why would he want to make an admission like that? Just to get me into his bed? A quick marriage, and a quick divorce? She hurled some expletives at him, out of anger.

'Names won't help,' he grandfather intervened. 'You go on home, young man. Come back tomorrow, and we'll set the date.'

'You can go on home now and never show your face around this place again,' she roared at him. 'Marry you? Because of a night on the bridge you expect me to marry you? Well, you can drop dead, Mr James Clarke. And get out of my house!'

Through her tears she could hear her grandfather escort him to the door. 'And it's *my* house, and *my* granddaughter,' the old man said, just a little more loudly than necessary, as he shut the door. In the living room Samantha let the tears roll. Tears of anger, and frustration.

Her grandfather came back and sat down opposite her, saying nothing, loading his pipe. His chair rocked in accompaniment to her tears, on and on. Why, she kept asking herself. Why in the world would he lie like that? If he *wanted* to marry me, said 'I love you,' I would have jumped at the chance. But like this? A shotgun wedding? How in the world could they expect my pride to stand up to that? Especially after nothing happened. Nothing! The tears gradually dried. She fished a tissue from the box on the coffee table, and dabbed at her eyes. When she looked up he was waiting for her, pipe cupped between both his hands.

'Why, Grandpa?' she asked. 'Why? Nothing happened!'

The old man sighed and shifted his weight in the chair. 'It ain't always what's happened, Samantha, but what people *think* has happened that's important. I been living in Rochester, man and boy, for seventy years or more. Your father was born and raised here. Your mother married here. You were born here. We have a name to uphold. What you done might not seem wrong to you, but it will *be* wrong in the community. Do you think you could live here, under a cloud like that? You think Vicky wouldn't suffer from it, with all her friends makin' remarks at the school, and their mothers doing their best to keep her away from their kids? You think your Ma and your Pa wouldn't suffer? Me, it wouldn't bother. I'm too old and crotchety to let it get to me—mind you, I ain't saying it wouldn't hurt, cause it would. So, shall we all pack up and move away? This here's no time for you to be thinking just of yourself, Samantha. You have to think of your family, too. Especially think of Vicky. And besides, I've been watching you. You sort of favour that boy anyway, don't you?'

She lifted a tear-streaked face to him, a solemn bitter face. He watched her anxiously. 'Perhaps once,' she said, 'but that's all gone now.' Something, a look of aching concern, and disappointment, flashed across his face and was instantly smothered.

'Them's fine words,' he grunted, 'But fine feathers don't make fine birds. You go on up and get some more rest. Tomorrow we'll go talk to your mother. And we'll have the wedding in, oh, two weeks.'

'We certainly will not!' And with that last grating bit of defiance Sam scrambled for the stairs. Beauty was waiting for her there. They both rushed in the bedroom, where she whirled around, dropped to the floor and hugged the dog close to her. 'Oh, Beauty,' she moaned, 'What am I going to do?' The dog licked at her nose, then gradually pushed at her until they were both lying on the rug, intertwined, communing with each other across the species-gap.

When she came downstairs the next morning she was exhausted after a sleepless night. But she saw Vicky and her grandfather with new eyes. The little girl was whistling away as she scrambled eggs for all of them. Eight years old, and already a victim of a terrible pounding from fate. Could her tender psyche stand up to another beating, one that might crumple her sustaining faith in her new mother? And the old man. Bent from burdens of more generations than his own, struggling as best he could to maintain a toe-hold on the land, on the town that he loved. But to solve their problems by a forced marriage? Sam shook her head stubbornly, and refused to accept it.

The three of them made a trip up to Boston in a new car, one Sam had never seen before. 'I bought it with the sale money,' he told her. 'First new car I ever owned, Sam.' He was trying his best to cheer her up, but she found it impossible to respond. A time-bomb was ticking off the minutes in her mind. You're going to get married in two weeks—unless you make such a terrible fuss that they all withdraw. They can't force you to marry him. And then she thought again. The devil they can't. They *can* force you, not by yelling and screaming, but by applying the overwhelming weight of duty and love. Why me, God? There must be a thousand other girls he could marry! But no, just because we were trapped on that—that bridge, I have to marry him? In a pig's eye, I will!

But as soon as she saw her mother, stretched out on the bed, with full plaster casts extending from her hips downward, and that light of pain in her eyes, Samantha knew she was fighting a losing battle. Even the re-union with her father could not overcome the gloom. They all left her with her mother.

'Now then, come over here and sit by me.' Her mother patted the side of the bed. Samantha approached it as if it were a guillotine. This big loving woman was her mother. Who had suffered more than her share of pain already. Sam sniffed, and forced back the tears just in time.

'I'm not going to marry him, Mother. I'm not! I'm going to Providence and work at the *Gazette*.

'It's gone too far for that, Samantha. You spent the night alone, naked, with a man. I have a New England conscience too, you must know. And your father and I, your grandfather, *we* can't run off to Providence to hide from the gossip. You have to marry, love. How about Charlie?'

'No . . .' She stifled a sob in her handkerchief. 'He came to see me at the hospital. It was the newspaper story. His mother showed it to him as soon as he got back from Worcester. We—he—— He won't have me. I gave him back his ring.'

'In that case,' her mother sighed, 'it has to be Clarke. There isn't any other alternative.' A torrent of words swept over her bowed head, ringing peals of love and home and faith and duty. It went on and on, that soft sweet voice seemingly so gently, and all the while driving in spikes as if building a railroad. Sam sank back and let the whole thing wash over her, until her ear alerted her to a change of subject. Her mother was talking about a wedding gown, and somehow Samantha realised that the battle was lost without appeal. Where and how she could not quite say. All she knew was that she was drowning, drowning, and the only way to save herself was to say yes. So she said it, and then wondered why.

'And we can get that made up in a hurry, with a beautiful light blue colour, Sam. It will look fine against the altar flowers.'

And at that point, cornered by it all, Samantha turned at bay.

'It's my wedding, Mother,' she said firmly. 'And I intend to be married in white.'

'Samantha! How can you? Not in our church!'

'You don't believe a word I've told you, do you, Mother?' There was a certain sorrow in her voice. None of them believed her. None of them. And it was only then that she realised how lonely the world was going to be, marrying a man who didn't love her.

'I'm going to be married in white,' she said very steadily, 'And I'm not going to be married in church at all.'

She said it without inflection. Her mother stopped talking, and looked. 'Yes,' she said softly. 'As you wish, dear.'

Her father was waiting for her as she came out the door. His long lean arms surrounded her, and for the first time in days the world seemed sensible. 'I didn't know what they were up to,' he told her. 'It's ridiculous. You don't have to marry him, Samantha—unless you want to.'

'Thank you, Dad. Nothing happened.'

'I believe you,' he replied. 'You don't have to marry him.' For just a moment she felt better, free from the terrible burden she had been carrying. And then her mind went back to her mother, lying so painfully in that bed. And her grandfather, close to the end of his life, clinging to the old ways with all his strength.

'Yes I do, Daddy,' she sighed. 'But he'll get no joy of it.'

For the next two weeks things seemed to go on around her. Things in which she could feel no concern at all. James' sister appeared in the house. Another giant of a woman, and sharing his blond curly hair and blue eyes. Things happened when she spoke. She took over all the arrangements.

Samantha wandered in and out of the house, not really interested in what was going on. She wore a perpetually dazed look on her face, as if it pained her to breathe. She spoke to nobody except Vicky and the dog. She would get up in the morning, nibble at a piece of toast, shrug herself into her coat or raincape as needed, and wander off, down to her valley. The dog kept her company, watched over her. The building was rising at a phenomenal pace, but she was no longer excited by it. On occasions she would come back for lunch, and eat nothing.

James came twice, in the evening. At both occasions the family disappeared, leaving them alone in the living room. He tried to talk to her, recounting the events of his day. He was an articulate and humorous man. But nothing broke through Samantha's guard. She sat across from him, refusing to share the couch, her hands folded quietly in her lap, and said nothing. When he left the first time there was a worried frown on his face, and he managed a quick conference with his sister. After the second visit he gave up and stayed away.

Naturally, on the day of the wedding it rained. The ceremony was scheduled for a Saturday morning, at eleven. The house had been cleaned to perfection, and flowers festooned the living room. Her mother came down from the hospital in Boston the night before, able to move her legs now, but still confined to the wheel chair. The house looked beautiful in all its wedding decorations, but there was a feeling of *funeral* in the air.

As she changed into the white knee-length dress she had chose, Samantha kept away from the mirror. There was nothing she wanted to see. The virgin goes forth to the sacrifice, she thought dully, and she doesn't care. She brushed her hair the required one hundred strokes, refused all offers of help, but did ask Vicky to remain in her room and share with her. Instead of a bouquet she threaded a green garland into her gold-splattered hair. The dress itself was simple, close-fitting, with no adornments. Her only jewellery was the gold cross that Vicky had given her, suspended now between her breasts on a thin gold chain.

'You look beautiful, Mommy,' the girl offered tentatively. Sam turned and looked down at her. 'You too, darling,' she offered. 'Do you still feel as badly about me marrying Mr Clarke?'

'Yes, I do,' the child sighed. 'I wish you wouldn't. You don't hafta, do you?'

'I'm afraid I do have to,' Sam returned gravely. 'I can't explain it, love. Sometimes adults have to do things that they don't want to, for reasons that aren't too clear to children. But I don't want you to worry, my dear. He will never lay a hand on you. I promise you that. You're my little girl—and you always will be!'

'I'm not worried about that, Mom.'

'You aren't bothered by the idea that we'll be away?'

'No. You promised to come back for me. Where are you going?'

'I don't know, love.'

'He didn't tell you?'

'I didn't want to know, sweetheart.' And there was the nub of it. Downstairs she could hear the hum of voices, people gathering for the ceremony. From someplace she could hear her mother's cheerful voice, approving all the arrangements. And Samantha Clark, the bride, just didn't care to know.

Her father came for her at ten-forty-five. She took his

arm, as pale as a ghost, saying nothing at all.
'Samantha . . .' he started to say, and then stopped. She
turned her head away so he would not see the sorrow in
her eyes.

'There's nothing more to say,' she told him quietly.

'They all think it's for your good,' he said bitterly.

'There's nothing more to be said.' He shrugged his
shoulders, a defeated look on his face, and led her
downstairs. Her mother was sitting in her wheelchair at
the bottom. She could read the pain in her daughter's
eyes, and it was too much to bear. She turned her chair
and wheeled away.

There were only a few guests in the living room. His
family had turned out *en masse*. All big powerful
people, who made six seem like a crowd. Samantha had
stubbornly refused to invite her friends. The group was
completed by a few neighbours, invited by her mother.

The ceremony was short. The words spoken, the
promises made, and his ring on her finger. Maybe it's
not me, she whispered to herself. Maybe it's some other
girl. Through it all she maintained her calm, saying
nothing that was not required of her, except the refrain
running through her mind, *He doesn't love me!* He
stooped to kiss her, but she evaded his lips. She would
have run, but his hand was on her elbow, and there was
no escape.

The ultra-solemn ceremony degenerated into a party.
Champagne, oysters on the half-shell, boiled lobster,
clams. All the product of the sea, that made the area
what it was. Tensions relaxed, and people began to talk.

With his hand compelling her, Samantha toured from
group to group, nodding gently at the conversations,
but saying nothing herself. Her presence, face grave,
eyes threatening to cry, dampened every group's
enthusiasm. By two o'clock the rain had stopped, the
clouds as empty as the champagne bottles. He was
called to help find more bubbly.

As soon as he moved away Samantha made a dead
set for the hall, ignoring her mother's call and her
grandfather's warning look. From the hook beside the

door she took down her old poncho and threw it over her wedding dress. The conversation behind her continued without let. She opened the front door and went out into the wet world.

There was a rainbow climbing the hills to the west. A brilliant clear rainbow, that matched the beautiful clean air. There was a nip of autumn in it all. She inhaled, and it raised her spirits. High up overhead, a long V-formation of ducks were heading south. She sauntered slowly around the barn and sat herself down on the wet bench that stood behind it. Her eyes were focused on the land. Focused, but saw nothing. His voice, coming from just behind her left shoulder, startled her.

'Samantha?' She turned her head slightly in his direction, and then looked away. He came around in front of her, tilting her chin up with one finger. 'Samantha, have I made such an unholy mess of it all?'

She stared at him, her huge eyes glistening.

'I feel like the world's worst fool,' he sighed. 'Your mother is crying her heart out, and your grandfather is hitting the bottle.'

'Why?' she asked fiercely. 'Why did you do it?'

'Because I was afraid it was the only way I could have you,' he answered gruffly. 'You were growing farther away from me every minute. I thought sure I had lost you to Aikens, and I couldn't stand that.'

'You couldn't stand losing?' she asked bitterly.

'No—it wasn't that way, Samantha. Not the way you're thinking. I need you. Need you and love you. You're the only girl I've ever felt this way about. And I know there won't be another one in ten thousand years. I need you badly. When your grandfather said—what he said—it seemed like manna from heaven for me. I thought I could love you enough for both of us, and I just grabbed at it. I need you. I love you!'

'So you split my family, made my mother my enemy, and ruined my reputation, because of your selfish need.' She could see the look of astonishment forming on his face.

He *loves* me? Have I had it all wrong, all this time?

Her mind raced, and a look of horror swept over her face. He interpreted it wrongly. He stumbled over to the bench and sat down beside her, just far enough away to avoid contact. She watched him out of the corner of her eyes as she berated her own stupidity. He's the same man as before, he looks the same, talks the same—and says he loves me! And you, Sam? Be honest. You've loved him all this time. Loved him mightily. Well, what's changed? Only the knowledge that your mother and grandfather have so little faith in you that they forced you to marry him! Ah, there's where it sticks, doesn't it. *Forced* to marry him. Not from strength, that force, but from weakness. Smothering your own needs, burying your own pride. Now there! That's the word. Pride! And now he says he loves you.

It's your pride, Samantha, that's sticking in your craw, choking you half to death. Take a look around you, little fool. Where are you now? Married to him, aren't you? Just the place you really wanted to be. No doubt about that! And you're jibing at it, making a chicken's neck of yourself, because of the *way* it happened, not *what* happened. Pride. What a cold bedfellow that will make over the years. If you turn him away now, what chance is there that you will ever meet his like again? None, of course. Absolutely none. Now look, Sam, her subconscious mind declared, I'll lay it all out for you. You loved him. You still love him. You wanted to marry him. You are married to him. Put your pride in your pocket and get on with life. He loves you!

She put her hand on his forearm, bemused by the droplets of water standing on the sleeve of his formal coat. 'James?'

He stood up and looked down at her. 'Alright Samantha,' he sighed. 'I've made a terrible mistake, and I shall suffer for it all my life. But I was so—I love you and need you Sam. I'll tell your father to start annulment procedures right away. May I kiss you goodbye?'

'No, you may not,' she stated firmly. 'It would have

been so easy, James. But with all this conniving and manoeuvring, you almost made me lose sight of the important thing—the only important thing. If you really love me, James, why don't you just ask? You've never *asked* me to marry you, you know.'

His eyes lit up, and he took a step closer. 'You really mean that, Sam. Even now?'

'Even now.' She shook both her hands out from under the poncho and reached up to him. He swept her off her feet and swung her around, kissing her gently and thoroughly.

It was a solemn wedding party, most of them sitting quietly in corners, who heard the front door bang, and the groom entered, carrying the bride in his arms. Both their faces were alight with warmth and love.

'Mr Hendricks!' James carried her across the room to where the Congregational minister was doing his best to keep up with the news of Mrs Clapton's jonquils, while at the same time trying to find some reasonable excuse to leave.

'Mr Hendricks. Samantha and I want to get married.'

'But I just married you.'

'That one won't do. We have to do it again.'

'Samantha, is that what *you* want?' the minister asked. He had to be sure. This certainly was not the same girl. The other one, the solemn pale little creature, had been replaced by a blushing, smiling bride. So he had to be sure.

'Of course that's what I want,' the bride said cheerfully. And so the wedding party was re-assembled. They wheeled her mother up close beside her, and Samantha squeezed her hand. The service was just as short, just as solemn, but there was a sparkle of happiness about the whole affair, and the sun, breaking through the clouds completely, gleamed through the west windows and silhouetted the young couple as they turned to kiss each other.

They both moved away from the improvised altar, and the groom swung his bride up in his arms again, heading for the door. There was a small problem. His dog and his new daughter, having waited patiently all this time, moved at just the wrong moment, sending the groom and his bride tumbling into a laughing heap in the hallway. The bride came up for air with her nose just inches away from her daughter's.

'I love him, Vicky,' she whispered in the girl's ear. 'Please don't be angry with me.'

'I'm not, Mommy,' the little girl chuckled. 'He's gotta catch me before he can pound me—and he's not much of a runner!'

CHAPTER THIRTEEN

It took another thirty minutes, and two more champagne toasts, before they were off again. The ground was still wet, so he carried her from the door to his car. A very conservative Buick, she noted. 'Loving a Ferrari is like loving a wife,' he lectured her. 'It's a once in a lifetime thing! And besides, I've got a family to support now.'

'Darned if you haven't,' she laughed. 'Can you afford us?'

'Us?'

'Vicky, Beauty, and me?'

'I'll make no promises, but I'll try very hard.' He waved to the celebration behind them, still going on, and gunned the car out on to the highway.

'How far are we going,' she inquired, trying to be casual about it all.

'Well, I thought I would rent the bridge for a week,' he said, 'but the State was having no part of that! We'll only be a minute.'

They went about two hundred yards up the road, to where a new sideroad had been recently bulldozed. He turned off the pavement, on to the dirt, and slowed. 'Even my driving has become more conservative,' he noted.

'Yes, of course,' she returned. But her thoughts were not on the conversation. She could feel an excitement building up in her as the new road swung around the hills she knew so well, past the cranberry bogs, and delivered them to the front steps of the building—the house—that she had watched for all these weeks.

'Here?' she asked, astonished. '*You* bought Grandpa's land?'

'Why of course I did. Who else? I hoped the first day

I met you that we would get married, and I would need a house. So I started one.'

'Started is the operative word, isn't it,' she laughed. 'The walls aren't finished yet, and the windows have to be put in. How in the world can we spend a honeymoon in an unfinished house?'

'Not to worry,' he assured her. 'Nobody knows we're here. There won't be a Peeping Tom within ten miles. This is all a big secret, and I've given the construction workers a week off.'

'But—the weather's turning cold, James.'

'Not with me around,' he laughed, 'and privacy is——'

His thoughts were interrupted by a loud wailing moan from up on the hill. Samantha burst out laughing. 'What in God's name is that?' he groaned.

'It's your dog,' she giggled. 'Our dog. We've been coming to watch the house a-building for the last few weeks. Nobody knows where we are, huh?'

'You mean I have to share my honeymoon with that monster?'

'Not a monster,' she assured him solemnly, 'A loving Beauty.'

'Yeah,' he groaned, as he watched the dog bound down the hill. 'Whereever in the world did you get that name, Beauty?'

'Oh, from an old childhood story,' she said demurely, and refused to add another word. He looked at her suspiciously, and then laughed at himself.

This is the time, she told herself. To tell him about Vicky. She moved over closer to him on the bench seat. 'James,' she said softly. 'Before we—before we go any further, I want to tell you about Vicky.'

He sealed off her lips with his finger. 'Don't say another word, love,' he said solemnly. 'Vicky is my daughter, and you are my wife. I don't want to know another single thing about it. Put it all behind you.' He replaced the finger with his lips, in a long satisfying kiss. It broke only when she had to come up for air, and all her determination was gone. Why spoil it, she sighed to herself. He'll find out soon enough, won't he? Just after he—Lord, I don't know what he's going to do! I've only read about it in books!

'Now listen, lady,' he laughed. 'This is my wedding day. Our wedding day, excuse me. The house isn't ready. I thought we had a month or more before the wedding. But that's what that house trailer is for. That's where we live until the house is finished.'

'And Vicky too?'

'Of course, Vicky too. I'm her father, aren't I? Now then, woman, I have assumed certain rights and responsibilities with you, and I aim to satisfy some of them right away. At once, do you hear?'

'Oh Lord, I hear alright,' she laughed. 'Another roarer in my life. I wonder how long it will take before I can finish the changes in my book. There's something I have to try out—it just *can't* be physically impossible!'

'Forget the book.' He was using a patented Groucho Marx leer, perhaps not too successfully. 'You'll have too much to do for the next month or so. There won't be time for the book.'

She carefully suppressed the idea of suggesting he might be boasting. She *was* learning, albeit slowly. He came around the car, opened her door, and picked her up. It's getting to be a habit with us, she told herself. I won't need my legs any more. He's going to carry me for the rest of my life!

'What the devil are you giggling about?'

'Just a passing thought. Don't trip over the dog. Why are you in so much of a hurry?'

'Lord, Samantha, I can't *tell* you, I have to *show* you. All the pleasures of the world are waiting for us, and I want it all so badly I can taste it!' The dog barked at him, somewhere between a doggish leer and a jeer, and moved out of the way.

Samantha nibbled at the closest ear. 'Boy, what a surprise you've got coming,' she told him. And giggled, somewhat apprehensively, all the way to the bedroom.

Hello!

You've come to the end of this story and we truly hope that you enjoyed it.

If you did (or even if you didn't!), have you ever thought that you might like to try writing a romance yourself?

You may not know it, but Mills & Boon are always looking for good new authors and we read every manuscript sent to us. Although we are proud to say that our standards are high and we can't promise every aspiring author success, unless you try you'll never know whether one of those new authors could be you!

Who knows, from being a reader you might become one of our well-loved authors, giving pleasure to thousands of readers around the world. In fact, many of our authors were originally keen Mills & Boon readers who thought, "I can do that" — and they did! So if you've got the love story of the century bubbling away inside your head, don't be shy: write to us for details today, sending a stamped addressed envelope. We'd really like to hear from you!

The Editors

Please write to:

Editorial Dept
Mills & Boon Ltd
15-16 Brook's Mews
London W1A 1DR

ROMANCE

Mills & Boon
COMPETITION

How would you like a year's supply of Mills & Boon Romances ABSOLUTELY FREE?

Well, you can win them!

All you have to do is complete the word puzzle below and send it into us by 31st August 1985. The first five correct entries picked out of the bag after that date will each win a year's supply of Mills & Boon Romances (Ten books every month—worth over £100!). What could be easier?

```
M R E T T E L T W I N M
B I T T E R O O R E H A
N C L H A Y V N E E R R
O I G L R S E E E S O R
S T U O S E S S I K D I
O O H Q F A E R T A O A
R X M T E C N S Y N A G
E E N R N L U D A C I E
A F F A I R R M B R P E
L O M E T E O A L O G W
M O E H A W I S H A O E
R L N M D E S I R E S N
```

Mills and Boon	Letter	Envy	Hug
Harlequin	Love	Rage	Men
Romance	Rose	Exotic	Hero
Tears	Wish	Girls	Heart
Bitter	Hope	Vow	Win
Daydream	Trust	Woman	Desires
Affair	Kisses	Eros	Realm
Marriage	Fool	Woe	

PLEASE TURN OVER FOR DETAILS ON HOW TO ENTER ⟹

How to enter

All the words listed overleaf, below the word puzzle, are hidden in the grid. You can find them by reading the letters forwards, backwards, up or down, or diagonally. When you find a word, circle it, or put a line through it. After you have found all the words, the left-over letters will spell a secret message that you can read from left to right, from the top of the puzzle through to the bottom.

Don't forget to fill in your name and address in the space provided and pop this page in an envelope (you don't need a stamp) and post it today. Hurry — competition ends 31st August 1985.

Mills & Boon Competition,
FREEPOST,
P.O. Box 236,
Croydon,
 Surrey CR9 9EL.

Secret message —————————————————————

Name —————————————————————————

Address —————————————————————————

—————————————————————————————

—————————————————————————————

————————————————— Postcode —————

COMP 1